STARLIGHT AT
MOONGLOW

STARLIGHT AT MOONGLOW

A Moonglow Christmas Novella

DEBORAH GARNER

CRANBERRY COVE PRESS

Cranberry Cove Press
PO Box 1671
Jackson, WY 83001, United States

Library of Congress Catalog-in-Publication Data Available
Garner, Deborah
Starlight at Moonglow / Deborah Garner—1st United States edition
1. Fiction 2. Woman Authors 3. Holidays

p. cm.
ISBN-13:
978-0-9969961-9-8 (paperback)
978-1-952140-19-8 (hardback)

Printed in the United States of America
10 9 8 7 6 5 4 3 2

For my mother,
who always made holidays special for us.

Books by Deborah Garner

The Paige MacKenzie Mystery Series

Above the Bridge
The Moonglow Café
Three Silver Doves
Hutchins Creek Cache
Crazy Fox Ranch
Sweet Sierra Gulch

The Moonglow Christmas Novella Series

Mistletoe at Moonglow
Silver Bells at Moonglow
Gingerbread at Moonglow
Nutcracker Sweets at Moonglow
Snowfall at Moonglow
Yuletide at Moonglow
Starlight at Moonglow

The Sadie Kramer Flair Series

A Flair for Chardonnay
A Flair for Drama
A Flair for Beignets
A Flair for Truffles
A Flair for Flip-Flops
A Flair for Goblins

Cranberry Bluff

ONE

Asharp wind hit Mist's face as she opened the front door of the Timberton Hotel and stepped out onto the porch. She, along with the rest of the townsfolk, had been hoping the storm would clear up before the Christmas holiday arrived. Instead, the skies remained obscured, and the freezing temperatures and heavy winds urged people back inside buildings. It was far from the peaceful coexistence between the inside world and Mother Nature that Mist wished for. Still, on a chilly, late-December morning like this, there was beauty in the tempestuous weather, a hidden promise that something better lay ahead.

Mist stepped back inside the hotel and closed the door softly. Stormy skies or not, guests would arrive later, and she still had much to prepare. Only so much could be done in advance; last-minute tasks always remained.

She fixed herself a cup of peppermint tea and took a seat at the center island in the kitchen. It was one of her favorite spots in the old hotel, a simple rectangular counter at which plans were created, conversation was shared, and small miracles managed to fall into place.

Taking a sip of tea, she opened the registration book and surveyed the list of incoming guests. All the regulars would be back. Clara Winslow and her husband, Andrew, would arrive that afternoon, as would several first-time guests. Nigel, known to everyone as "the professor," would show up early the following day, the eve of Christmas Eve. And Michael Blanton, with whom Mist had developed a lovely romantic connection over the past few years, would arrive later that same afternoon. It warmed her heart to know all the return guests would be present for the hotel's traditional holiday activities, including Betty's cookie exchange and Mist's much-loved Christmas Eve dinner.

Mist ran a finger down the list of names, lingering on Michael's. He had seemed preoccupied lately when they talked, but she knew he was busy preparing for outreach classes to start after the new year. He'd be coordinating the local program, which meant—much to her delight—that he'd be in town frequently, and they'd be able to spend more time together.

She let her finger continue down the page in a soft, swirling motion, letting her gaze linger a few seconds on each additional name, those of guests who'd be spending their first Christmas holiday at the hotel.

"Working your magic on the reservation book?"

Looking up, Mist smiled at the sight of Betty entering through the kitchen's back door. The hotelkeeper was barely recognizable amid the multiple layers of wool needed to guard against the fierce weather outside. Two eyes and a nose peeked out below a thick knit cap, and a burgundy wool scarf covered the woman's mouth, slightly muffling her words.

"Doing my best," Mist said as she stood to help Betty pry off multiple layers of clothing. Once vest, jacket, gloves, hat, scarf, and snow boots had all been set aside, she fixed another cup of tea, and both women took places at the counter.

"We'll have a full house this year, as usual." Betty blew across the cup of tea, took a careful sip, and sighed. "Ah... a hot beverage is wonderful after tackling that storm out there. Thank you."

Mist smiled and shook her head. "You know I would have been glad to run those cookies down to Clive for you so you wouldn't have to go out in the cold."

Betty waved the comment away with one hand. "Nonsense. With everything you need to do to get ready for our guests? I wouldn't think of it. You always have your hands full at this time of year, though you also have everything under control. I don't know how you do it."

"We all do it," Mist pointed out. "You bake those delicious, glazed cinnamon nuts that everyone is addicted to, Clive makes sure we have plenty of firewood, and Maisie provides us with beautiful flowers from her shop. We work together to make the holidays special for our guests."

"I guess you have a point there," Betty said. "Speaking of flowers, Maisie was just dropping off your order as I walked up. She thinks you'll be pleased with the assortment. She said to tell you she left them in the café."

Mist's eyes lit up, always delighted with a chance to create arrangements with what she viewed as nature's gifts. "Wonderful. Is she still here? I'd like to thank her."

Betty shook her head. "She needed to get home to watch Clay Jr. so Clayton could get to his office in the fire station."

"Of course. I'll stop by the flower shop and thank her later."

"Remind me who we have coming this year, aside from the regulars." Betty reached across the countertop and tapped the registration book. "If I recall, we have some interesting people coming."

Mist smiled. "Each one of us is unique. So, you are right, this will be a wonderful group of guests, just as it is every year." She looked over the list and recited notes she'd made when taking the reservations. "Nora Wallace will be arriving from Atlanta, Georgia, with her young daughter, Whitney. Dr. Daniel Hutton—an elderly man, perhaps, according to his voice—will join us from Saint George, Utah. And Steven Mitchell and his wife, Erika, are traveling all the way from Nova Scotia to spend the holiday here. He's hearing-impaired, and his wife functions as his interpreter, which should be quite fascinating." She closed the book, set it aside, and remained quiet.

"I know that contemplative look of yours," Betty said. "You've just thought of something."

"You're right," Mist said. "Or, more accurately, of someone."

"Hollister." Betty's expression indicated she knew she was right, and it was the logical guess. The formerly homeless man had never spoken and was oblivious to sound around him. They'd long known he couldn't hear, even years before when he slept under the town's railroad trestle. With Mist's gentle encouragement, he now slept in a back hotel room that hadn't been used for years. It had been a simple matter of putting in a bed and a refrigerator, ostensively a backup for the hotel. Mist always managed to keep the fridge stocked with food, and the exterior door to the room unlocked.

"Yes, Hollister." Mist lightly tapped her fingertips on the counter's surface. "Perhaps a bit of holiday magic is coming our way."

"I don't doubt it," Betty said. "Some of that magic seems to come around every Christmas here in Timberton."

Mist smiled. "Yes. And I believe this year will be no different."

TWO

Of all the spots within the Timberton Hotel that Mist loved, the closet in the back hallway was her favorite, or at least one of her favorites, as there were many she loved the most. If asked, she would say there was no reason to only have one *most*, that *most* was infinite. Still, this closet was special, as it held the trinkets and tidbits that she collected whenever she found something unique or whimsical or lovely in some way, something that spoke to her heart, even for unknown reasons.

Stepping inside the closet always felt like entering a magical kingdom, a world of possibilities. And she did feel that was the case because random items placed in guest rooms had the potential of inspiring those who saw them, touched them, or held them.

Mist slid a metal box off a low shelf and set it on the floor. Lifting the lid, she reached in and brought out one of several tin soldiers. While only three inches tall, it spoke to her of strength and compassion, of steadfast loyalty. A small opening in its fist spoke of a missing item, a weapon, most likely. This she loved the most about the miniature figure; she had her own idea to fill the tiny space.

From other shelves, she pulled a vintage charm bracelet, a peacock feather, a jeweled cloisonné turtle, bits of bobbin lace, and a string of recycled glass beads. She was never quite sure which room would receive which of the items; she felt the items might pick their own homes as she made her way through the hotel, adding last-minute touches to the guest accommodations.

She gathered her choices into a basket and made her way to each room, leaving behind whatever object inspired her at the moment. The cloisonné turtle came to rest on an antique mahogany dresser; the lace settled into a rose-patterned china dish. An Eastlake oak mirror provided a place to hang the glass beads, and the tin soldier chose its own room, content to remain there with the peacock feather in its hand.

Pleased, Mist returned to the closet, put the basket away, and moved on to a bookcase toward the rear of the front parlor. Knowing Michael's love of reading, it was always a delightful task to choose an assortment of books to leave by his favorite reading chair. Classics being a favorite, she gathered John Milton's *Paradise Lost*, William Faulkner's *The Sound and the Fury*, Virginia Woolf's *To the Lighthouse,* and Jack London's *The Call of the Wild*. After setting them on the table by the fireplace, a wave of inspiration hit her, and she chose books to leave in each guest room, including copies of Madeleine Engle's *A Wrinkle in Time* and Elizabeth George Speare's *The Witch of Blackbird Pond*—favorites of her own when she was young—in the room for the mother and daughter.

Hearing conversation and laughter coming from the kitchen, she followed the voices and found Betty and

Clive at the center table, each with a cup of coffee, Clive with the additional treat of a slice of orange almond cake that Mist had baked that morning. As soon as she stepped into the room, Betty took a quick sip of coffee and Clive shoved a forkful of cake in his mouth.

"I had a feeling those were your voices I heard down the hallway," Mist said. "I'm glad to see you relaxing, Clive. You've been working too hard lately."

"It's a busy season," Betty said, eyeing Clive as she set her coffee down. "Isn't that right?"

Clive nodded as he returned her look, mouth still full.

Mist put a teakettle on the stove and took a seat across from them. "Running the gallery and remodeling at the same time is a lot to take on."

Clive swallowed and then shrugged. "I've been working on it little by little over the years."

"Since the café will be staying here in the hotel, you could wait to fix up the old building, enjoy the holiday now," Mist suggested.

"You have a good point, dear," Betty said, fiddling with her cup. "But this way he can get new tenants in soon after the first of the year. Those kitchen fixtures were never replaced after that fire years ago, so it won't be a restaurant. Not that any place could be competition for the Moonglow Café."

"Yes," Clive said between bites. "Something different."

"I'd love to see it," Mist said. "I have wonderful memories there." She turned to Betty. "Although the Timberton Hotel is definitely the café's home now."

"And we're delighted it is!" Betty said.

Clive cleared his throat. "No one's allowed in now. Construction zone, insurance regulations, all of that."

Mist nodded. "Well, I look forward to seeing it when it's done."

"I'll make sure you do," Clive said.

"And I'll make sure I keep baking so you'll take breaks."

"That's a deal that meets my approval!" Clive took a last bite, thanked Betty and Mist for the coffee and cake, and headed back to work.

"Anything for food." Betty chuckled as she moved Clive's empty cup and plate to the sink. "At least he's consistent."

"A wonderful trait," Mist mused, "especially if tempered with a touch of spontaneity."

Betty returned to her seat at the counter. "I'm glad he has help in the gallery this year. I've seen all the miniature paintings you've been sending down. They keep selling out. The new one with the fox in the snow is so popular."

"There's something especially appealing about foxes," Mist said. "It may be their eyes or their bushy tails or simply the fact they have an air of mystery about them."

"They're quite like cats, you know," a voice added to the conversation. "Their eyes are vertically slanted, they're nocturnal, and they pounce in a similar fashion to catch their prey."

Mist and Betty both turned toward the kitchen door, delighted to see Nigel Hennessy standing there.

"Professor!" Betty exclaimed. She greeted the familiar guest, giving him a hug, which he accepted awkwardly, in keeping with his proper disposition. "Welcome. You made it, driving down here from Missoula."

"Barely," the professor said. "I dare say the wind almost blew me off the road more than once. It's quite the dog's dinner out there!"

Mist smiled at the professor's British speech. In spite of moving to the United States to accept a university position five years ago, his London roots were ever apparent.

"Glad you made it safely," Clive said as he stood up to shake the professor's hand. "It wouldn't be Christmas here without you."

"It wouldn't be Christmas without a certain someone's Christmas Eve dinner."

"You're very kind," Mist said.

"And very honest," the professor said. "Shall I take my usual room?"

"Yes, and it's ready for you, complete with tea and biscuits. I'll bring a pot of hot water up in just a bit."

"Brilliant."

Mist filled the kettle she had put on the stove while Betty walked to the lobby with the professor to complete his hotel registration and give him a key. In only a few minutes, the water was boiling. Mist filled a china teapot and delivered it to the professor's room, along with his favorite teacup.

"Thank you, Mist," the professor said as he opened his door.

"You're welcome," Mist said. "We're delighted to have you with us for Christmas again."

It was true, Mist thought as she walked back to the kitchen. Welcoming return guests was one of the most delightful aspects of the holiday season. And, among those, seeing the professor each year was one of the biggest joys.

THREE

Mist lowered herself into a chair and looked at the foliage and blooms spread across the wooden table before her. Maisie had found an exquisite assortment this year: white roses and spider chrysanthemums, red tulips and delphinium, pale green hyacinth, winter berries, and branches of seeded eucalyptus and rosemary.

On a table to her left, a cluster of half-pint milk bottles rested beside a dozen handmade wooden crates, each measuring approximately six inches square. Mist was pleased with the containers for this year's arrangements, having found the milk bottles at an antique shop in Helena and the crates at a craft fair that Millie, the librarian, had recently held at the library. The crates would fit perfectly in the center of each café table; the petite milk bottles were to hold mixed assortments of flowers for each guest room.

Of the many facets she loved about Christmas, decorating sat high on the list, almost—but not quite—tied with preparing cuisine for guests and townsfolk and painting miniature canvases for gifts and galleries. Holiday traditions filled her with joy, a joy she loved sharing with all around her. Others often told her she created this for them, but she knew the truth: people created their own joy by inviting it in. Decorations, food, and art only opened the door.

Mist stood, her green rayon skirt swaying above worn work boots as she retrieved one of the crates. The four-inch height of the wooden sides provided exactly what she wanted: a rustic base for a low arrangement, which would allow those attending the hotel's Moonglow Café on Christmas Eve to see each other across the tables. The buffet along the side of the room would boast a taller display.

Stem by stem, Mist drew the "ingredients," as she was known to call such things, together into mosaics of petals and leaves, tucking them into shallow glass dishes that she placed inside each wooden crate. As she finished each one, she stood and circled the table, viewing the arrangement from all sides and adding a touch here and there—a tiny pine cone, perhaps, or an extra sprig of red berries. Finally she stood back and surveyed the festive creations. Pleased with how they looked, she gathered the remaining flowers and greenery into clusters and filled the small milk bottles. She then placed all the crates and bottles along the back of the buffet where they'd be out of the way until needed.

The sound of the café door opening preceded Betty's voice.

"Nora Wallace and her daughter are here to check in and… Oh my, those centerpieces are gorgeous!"

"Thank you, Betty. I just finished them." Mist smiled. "I think they'll set a festive tone."

"No question about that," Betty said. "I'll have Mrs. Wallace fill out the registration card, but I thought you'd like to greet them."

"Absolutely. I'll be right there." Mist set a small handful of pine cones aside and retreated to the kitchen to wash her hands, which bore traces of green from stems along with a small scratch from a rose thorn. Drying them with a kitchen towel, she joined Betty and the new arrivals in the hotel lobby.

"Welcome to the Timberton Hotel, Mrs. Wallace and..." Mist turned with equal spirit to the younger of the two. "...Ms. Wallace. We're so pleased to have you here."

"Please call us Nora and Whitney," Nora said. She set a pen down, having completed the registration, and then reached out affectionately toward her daughter, a twig of a girl not quite into her teens, accompanied by crutches. Mist noted a certain sadness in the girl's countenance, something beyond physical that she couldn't quite define.

"Nora and Whitney then. My name is Mist." She watched the daughter's expression turn puzzled at the sound of her unusual name, something she was used to. Just as quickly, the girl relaxed and smiled. "I help Betty here at the hotel," Mist added.

Betty chuckled. "Now there's an understatement if I ever heard one. If anything, I'm the one helping her."

"We all help each other," Mist clarified. She smiled at Betty, then turned back to the newly arrived guests. "You must be tired after traveling. How would you like me to show you to your room? It's just upstairs."

She looked at Whitney. "Will that be difficult for you? I'm so sorry. I didn't realize you'd be on crutches."

Whitney shook her head. "I can handle it."

"It just happened two days ago," Nora explained. "A sports injury during a dance team practice."

"I'm sorry, Whitney," Mist said. "That must hurt. Please let us know if we can help make things easier during your stay."

Nora reached for her suitcase, but Mist had swept it up quickly. Whitney attempted to lift her smaller travel bag's handle next to one crutch, but the weight made it too awkward. The trio ascended the staircase, three hands running along the polished wooden banister, and followed the hallway to a suite that Mist had felt—and now felt even more certain—would be perfect for the guests. With two rooms and a small common area between, the daughter could have some privacy if she wanted. Alternatively, the larger of the two bedrooms could easily accommodate both mother and daughter.

Options, Mist mused, just as she had told Betty when assigning the rooms. *Life is full of options.*

Hearing new activity below, Mist encouraged Nora and Whitney to settle in and then come downstairs for freshly baked chocolate chip cookies whenever they'd like. She returned to the lobby where, to her delight, she found Clara Winslow and her husband, Andrew, longtime guests of the hotel.

"Welcome!" Mist exclaimed. "We're delighted to have you back again. You both look well." She exchanged hugs with each of them.

"You know we wouldn't miss Christmas at the Timberton Hotel," Clara said. "And we brought you a little something this year from a trip we took to the Netherlands." She turned to her husband. "Andrew?"

Andrew pulled a looped ribbon from his pocket. On the end dangled a pair of wooden shoes approximately two inches in length. A sweet village scene graced the front of each shoe.

"How lovely!" Mist took the ornament and admired them. "This will be a wonderful addition to our tree, something for everyone to enjoy."

"Oh, I want to see this year's tree!" Clara exclaimed, looking toward the front parlor.

"Go look," Betty said, waving her on. "I'll finish up with Andrew."

Clara headed for the eight-foot Douglas fir framed by the hotel's front window. Andrew remained behind to finish registering. Pleased to hear they'd have their usual room, he reached for their luggage only to be stopped by a stern voice.

"Now, now, we'll have none of that carrying-your-own-bags business around here!"

"Clive, old guy, still a troublemaker, I see." Andrew chuckled as Clive grabbed one of the two bags. "How are you?"

"Not bad," Clive announced. "Betty and Mist keep me in line. I couldn't get in trouble if I wanted to these days."

"As it should be," Betty quipped.

"Anything you say, dear," Clive called out as he and Andrew disappeared with the bags.

Mist smiled, listening to the exchange between Betty and Clive. It always made her heart sing to hear the senior lovebirds' banter. Their lighthearted remarks created an atmosphere of joy around them that was contagious.

Betty sorted the remaining registration cards, those for guests who had yet to check in. She set them out in order of expected arrival and then turned to Mist. "I'm going to visit with Clara by the tree. Want to join us?"

"You go ahead," Mist said. "I hear the kitchen calling me. I'd better start dinner preparations if guests and townsfolk plan on eating tonight."

"Then by all means, go." Betty shooed Mist forward with the backs of both hands as if chasing chickens from the lobby.

Laughing, Mist headed to the kitchen, eager to see what culinary magic awaited. For it was all magic to her: the scent of cloves and oranges, the sweet taste of honey on fresh biscuits, the sight of a chocolate soufflé fresh from the oven, and the sound of people conversing over a good meal.

FOUR

With Christmas Eve dinner—a lavish affair—only forty-eight hours away, the evening meal on this particular day consisted of light fare. Mist made a point of offering simple meals on the days leading up to the traditional feast. Or at least they were simple, in her opinion. She preferred not to plan too precisely. This allowed her to gather the freshest ingredients available at any given time and use whatever inspiration followed.

Still, she followed a general guideline when choosing what to prepare for the buffet. Usually two main dishes—one for those who ate meat, another for those who didn't. A salad of sorts, whether mixed greens or something more exotic. A vegetable dish, two if the local produce offerings were so exquisite that she couldn't decide between them, and homemade rolls or bread. Dessert might be as simple as fresh fruit or as complex as any number of international pastries. The decision, like all culinary decisions she made, depended on available goods and mostly whim and fancy, including the matter of how the meal was served.

When hotel guests and townsfolk entered the café that evening, they found a long row of bowls stretching from one end of the buffet to the other. The serving dishes were similar but not identical, all made of glazed pottery but differing in size, shape, color, and design. They seemed primitive yet charming, and it soon became clear why. Mist had cleverly convinced a local school to offer a pottery program, and Michael had arranged for an art teacher from the university to volunteer instruction and supervision. The children each made two bowls, one to keep and one for a school fundraiser, the goods of which were immediately purchased by the hotel, the funds from which went straight back to the school for needed supplies.

"These are wonderful!" Clara exclaimed as she surveyed the long row of artistic serving dishes. "Such a variety! Look, Andrew, have you ever seen anything like this?"

Andrew leaned down, inspecting the glazed surfaces in fuchsia, emerald, rose, mustard, sage green, and more. "No, I can't say that I have."

"Polka dots and squiggles and lightning bolts." The professor, having followed Clara and Andrew into the café, surveyed the bowls' sides. "How very clever."

"I especially like the ones that are uneven around the top," Clara said. "The little imperfections make them even more delightful. They're all so unique, so individual."

"Like the children who created them," Mist explained, telling the guests the backstory. "They were only given basic instruction on the clay formation. Decorating was left to their imaginations. The university then fired the bowls in their art department's kilns and returned them here to the children."

"Quite keen," the professor said.

Clive's voice soon joined the conversation. "Even better, they have food in them!"

"The man does have his priorities, doesn't he, Nigel?" Andrew quipped.

"Indeed." The professor perused the offerings, starting at one end of the buffet and continuing to the other.

"My aunt used to serve this when we had large family gatherings," Mist said. "She called it a Bali dinner, a type of island buffet."

"Sounds intriguing," the professor said. "But I dare ask, how are we to eat this? What is the correct procedure?" He adjusted his glasses and contemplated the spread.

"Allow me to demonstrate." Mist took a plate from a stack on one end of the buffet and moved along the offerings, miming additions to her plate, each on top of the other, as she debated the choices aloud. "Rice, yes... crispy noodles, yes... chicken, not for me but perhaps for you... white cream sauce, yes... pineapple, yes... cheese, maybe not... slivered almonds, yes... peas, please... and on and on."

"On top of each other?" Nora asked, having just stepped in with Whitney. "Just like that?"

"Exactly," Mist said. "But only the items you'd like. Feel free to pass by anything that doesn't appeal to you."

"It looks like fun," Clara said, taking a plate and handing another to Andrew. She stepped along from bowl to bowl, choosing most items and reminding Andrew of his nut allergy as they came to the almonds.

Nora and Whitney followed, both making their way along the buffet. While Nora arranged layers on her plate, Whitney paid more attention to the bowls themselves, running her fingers along the sides of each, admiring the colors and designs.

Others dropped in for the meal as the dinner hour continued. Michael and Clive piled their plates high, hungry after working on Clive's building renovation project all day. Even William "Wild Bill" Guthrie admitted the spread was wilder than anything his greasy spoon down the road served.

Maisie came by, offering help as always, but Mist and Betty assured her that everything was under control. They encouraged her to relax and enjoy dinner with Clayton and Clay Jr., which she did. Several other townsfolk joined their table.

Back in the kitchen later, Betty gave Mist a thumbs-up for the unusual buffet. "They loved it, especially the fact they could pick and choose what they wanted. And the coconut sorbet for dessert was perfect. Not to mention the music you had playing. I can't remember the last time I heard Bing Crosby and the Andrews Sisters sing 'Mele Kalikimaka.'"

"I thought something a little different would be fun tonight," Mist said. "I'm delighted everyone enjoyed it."

"I'd certainly call it a success," Betty said. "Clive had seconds if not thirds. I think he just enjoyed piling each layer on top of the one before. Then again, the professor... Did you see his plate?"

Mist grinned. "Yes, I saw it."

"We might have expected he'd portion each ingredient out into separate locations on his plate." Betty chuckled. "He does like things a particular way."

Mist nodded. "I find it admirable. Orchestrating life to one's preferences is an art."

"Speaking of art, those bowls were a fantastic way to serve everything. The buffet looked like a picture from a magazine. So colorful and appealing."

"Presentation offers flavor beyond that within the food. Flavor is more than just what we taste; it's what we experience."

"I never thought of it that way," Betty said. "But I suppose you're right. If we'd served everything in plastic containers instead of those lovely bowls, it might not have tasted the same."

"It might have tasted the same, but people's perception of that taste would have been different. So, in that sense, it *wouldn't* have tasted the same." Mist turned her palms up, as if resting her case.

"Are we philosophizing again in here?" Clive teased them as he entered the kitchen with a stack of plates. "And just who might have started that?" He set the plates down on the main counter.

"Someone needs to keep us thinking," Michael added, following Clive into the room. He exchanged a sweet kiss with Mist and then added a second batch of plates to those Clive had brought in. Two more round trips by both men managed to gather the rest of the dinner dishes.

"Now I *am* going to help," Maisie said, joining the others in the kitchen. "Clayton took Junior home, and this is my excuse to linger." She stepped over to the sink and turned the water on, feeling the temperature with one hand as it warmed up.

"Thank you," Betty said. "I don't know what we'd do without you, Maisie."

"You're welcome," Maisie said as she picked up a dish from one of the stacks. "Though I'm sure Clive would have been glad to do the dishes instead."

"Uh… right!" Clive said. "I would have loved to, but I wouldn't want to take that pleasure away from Maisie." Mist noticed him wink at Betty, which she found charming.

FIVE

The hotel was quiet when Mist slipped into the kitchen from the back hallway the following morning. She was used to being the first one awake in the building, and she relished the peacefulness of the early hours. The routine that accompanied the start of a new day felt soothing and familiar, as well it would after years. She would set up coffee in the lobby, always having it ready by six thirty when she knew Clive would sneak into the hotel for the first cup of the day. Once coffee was brewing, she'd slide a pan or tray into the oven, perhaps pumpkin bread, perhaps lemon-poppyseed muffins, or perhaps some impulsive combination of dry ingredients, butter, fruit, and spices. As the aroma of the fresh baking filled the kitchen, she'd set the buffet up with fresh juices, a fruit platter, and a main breakfast dish of some kind.

And so it was that guests and townsfolk arrived at the café in the morning to find a sun-dried-tomato-and-cheese frittata, a bowl of mixed berries, and a basket of cranberry-orange mini-muffins. Although first-timers were surprised at this, return guests and locals knew each morning brought a delightful meal to start the day. The fact there were no menus just made the meal easier to enjoy whether half-awake or half-asleep. Townsfolk contributed; hotel guests had meals included with their lodging. Mist's Pay What Your Heart Tells You sign made the meal affordable for everyone. Somehow the payment for meals always covered what was needed to keep providing sustenance to all.

It never surprised Mist or Betty—or anyone really—that Clayton and his fire workers were the first to grab a table. They ate heartily, which was not only encouraged but appreciated. Everyone knew they worked hard to keep the town safe. Montana was no stranger to fires, and Clayton's crew always stood ready.

The professor, Clara, and Andrew were the next to take breakfast seats, sitting together to catch up on whatever had happened since the Christmas before. Nora and her daughter entered, choosing a table for two, and the remaining hotel guests soon followed.

"Is Michael having breakfast?" Betty asked Mist as she brought an orange juice pitcher into the kitchen to refill. "I haven't seen him."

"He's helping Clive today, but he said he'd stop by."

"That's good," Betty said. "I'm sure Clive can use the help."

"It'll be a good distraction for Michael," Mist said. "It should help take his mind off the outreach program."

"Maybe this will help them both calm down so they can enjoy Christmas Eve and Christmas Day," Betty suggested.

"I hope so," Mist mused.

Dr. Daniel Hutton arrived shortly after breakfast ended. A thin, almost frail, soft-spoken man, he was younger than Mist had expected from his voice on the phone. While she'd pegged the voice as elderly, Daniel Hutton looked no more than fifty. He filled out the registration card and quietly excused himself to rest, citing a difficult drive that had fortunately delivered him safely to the hotel. White-knuckled his way in, he explained, as heavy wind had battered his rental car from side to side and falling snow had continually obscured the windshield.

Steven and Erika Mitchell soon followed, completing the arrival of new guests. They'd also fought their way through the storm, although a sturdy four-wheel-drive vehicle had helped them maneuver the roads. Steven had watched Mist attentively as she welcomed them, and she realized he was adept at reading lips. Erika additionally translated with sign language, which Mist observed with equal attention, charmed with the process of communication between the three of them. Steven registered for them, completing the hotel form with precise penmanship. Mist escorted them to their room and invited them to join others in the parlor after they settled in.

Retreating to the kitchen, she found Betty taking care of the breakfast dishes. To her delight, Michael, who, after many visits between holidays, had grown comfortable with inner hotel habits, sat at the center island with a mug of coffee. Mist circled around and greeted him from behind with an affectionate hug, during which he snuck a gentle kiss on her neck.

Betty smiled, observing the exchange while drying the platter that had held the melon earlier, and sighed. "You two make such an adorable couple."

"Well," Michael said. "I can't speak for myself, but the other half of this couple is adorable, without a doubt."

Mist, never quite as easy receiving compliments as giving them, blushed as she attempted to join Betty's efforts to clean up from the morning meal.

"Don't even try to help," Betty mock-scolded with a grin. "You prepared the meal, and I know perfectly well you'll be catering to guest needs all day, not to mention feeding the masses again later. I've got this. Besides, I want to make more of those glazed cinnamon nuts. Nora's daughter seems to have a sweet tooth, although I noticed she barely ate enough for a sparrow at breakfast."

"Maybe too many of those nuts," Michael suggested.

"I'm not sure about that," Mist said. "I noticed she ate very little at dinner last night too. I suspect there's something on her mind. Besides, I wouldn't blame anyone in particular for that bottomless candy dish. You know the neighborhood teens sneak in every year for those treats."

"That's true," Michael said. "It's quite a mystery, the veritable Bermuda Triangle of glazed cinnamon nuts."

"Perhaps Whitney will feel like talking at some point," Mist said.

"If she'll talk to anyone, it'll be you," Betty said. "People have a way of opening up to you."

Mist smiled. "It's not about me; it's about listening. Most people simply want someone to listen. Not a solution, not advice. Just someone to listen to what they have to say."

The kitchen door swung open, and Clive stuck his head in. "I restocked the firewood, so you should be set for several days."

"Thank you, Clive," Mist said. "Those lovely fires are so soothing. That and some soft Christmas music."

"You have a point," Betty said. "I can almost see people relax physically when they're in that front parlor with firelight and music."

"It's true," Michael said. "I've experienced it many times, sitting by the fireplace. Your muscles relax. Your body relaxes."

Clive continued to stand in the doorway, much like a dog waiting for a treat. Amused, Mist took a chocolate chip cookie from a cookie jar and walked over to him. "Sit," she said with a twinkle in her eyes. Betty and Michael both snickered in the background.

"Very funny." Clive took the cookie and excused himself to get back to work.

"I'd better go help him." Michael stood up and carried his coffee mug to the sink. "Do I get a cookie too?"

"I suppose that's fair." Mist took several cookies from the jar and placed them in a reusable container. "And some extras for later."

"Don't let Clive get too close to those, or you might not get any for yourself." Betty grinned.

"You may share them with anyone you wish." Mist added a few more cookies.

After Michael left, Mist turned to Betty. "I don't think Whitney is the only guest with something occupying her mind. Daniel Hutton was very quiet when he checked in."

"I noticed that," Betty said. "I do hope he's okay."

"Perhaps he also needs someone to listen," Mist suggested. "Or he may just need time alone with his thoughts. I suppose we'll see."

"This is your 'all in due time' mode," Betty said. "I recognize it."

"Yes. Life has its own timing."

SIX

Although Mist remained in the hotel whenever Betty hosted her yearly cookie exchange, she made a point of staying in the background—available if needed but otherwise observing from afar. This was the one time during the holidays that Betty had a chance to shine on her own, which was only fair. She'd started the annual event long before Mist came to Timberton.

"How do I look?" Betty turned in a circle as Mist sat at the kitchen's center counter and took in the hotelkeeper's attire. She'd dressed up for the event this year, even donning a black wool gabardine skirt and low-heeled dress shoes. Her elegant red sweater featured a cheerful Santa Claus face, its swirling white beard heavily embellished with beads and sequins. Both the skirt and sweater had been recent arrivals at Second Hand Sally's, and Mist knew Betty had been counting the days until she could show the outfit off. And for good reason; she looked fantastic.

"Absolutely beautiful!" Mist said. "Has Clive seen you yet?"

Betty shook her head. "No, but I suspect he'll be around before long. Where there are cookies, there's Clive."

"Indeed." Mist laughed. "You can count on that."

"Oh! I hear the front door!" Betty's face lit up like a child hosting a birthday party. "Come with me, Mist. Let's see who's brought what!"

Enchanted by Betty's enthusiasm, Mist followed her out to the café, which had been rearranged for the cookie exchange, dining tables brought together to form one long row. Mist's floral centerpieces sat at regular intervals down the middle, leaving the rest of the surface free for platters of baked delights.

A stack of circular wire baskets waited at one end, an assortment of oversized quilting squares beside them. Betty had been thrilled with the idea of the basket and fabric combination as Mist collected remnants during the course of the year. Together they had trimmed the sides with pinking shears. Half the squares featured holiday patterns—holly branches, snowflakes, candy canes—while others boasted a variety of designs to use anytime of the year. Participants could line their baskets with whichever whimsical prints spoke to them, and they would be encouraged to choose two— one a holiday theme, a second, hidden underneath, to use other times of the year.

Marge, Betty's dear friend and owner of the town's candy shop, entered first, followed right behind by Sally, who ooh'd and aah'd over Betty's outfit. Both women had shed snow-covered outerwear in the main lobby on their way in. Their festive attire was paired with slightly wayward hair from heavy knit hats.

"I don't remember ever having weather this crazy at Christmas before," Marge said as she set a plate of maple nut fudge on the table.

Mist smiled. "As Helen Keller said, 'Life is a daring adventure or nothing.'"

"Well, this storm is definitely a daring adventure!" Marge said.

"That outfit was meant for you, Betty!" Sally said as she placed a tin of almond shortbread next to Marge's fudge.

Betty repeated the spin she'd performed for Mist in the kitchen. "Thank you, Sally. What would we do without your wonderful thrift shop?"

"Here, here," Millie said. "I'd have to wear pajamas every day if not for you, Sally." She added a platter of rhubarb cookies to the other offerings. "I hope I'm not late. We had a last-minute rush at the library with people wanting extra books to read over the holiday. It took longer than usual to close up."

"You're right on time," Betty said, scurrying off to meet other townsfolk as they entered. Before long, the cookie exchange was overflowing with sweet treats of all kinds. Clive, to no one's surprise, passed through and turned on all the charm he could muster in exchange for a few "taste tests" as he called it.

Mist leaned toward Betty and whispered, "I'll leave you to enjoy the cookie exchange. I'm going to run down to see Maisie at her shop. She's working on last-minute orders."

"That's fine, dear," Betty said. "I see the ginger crisps she dropped off earlier. Thanks for adding those to the table." She turned to greet Glenda from the Curl 'n' Cue, the beauty salon just behind the billiards section of Pop's Parlor, the local watering hole.

Taking a jacket from the front closet, Mist zipped it up and pulled the faux fur-trimmed hood over her head. Facing the blustery weather, she walked down to Maisie's Daisies, where she found Maisie buried in fresh blooms and foliage. A few eucalyptus leaves dotted her florist friend's shoulders, and a sprig of baby's breath stuck out of her holiday-appropriate green hair.

"You look like a flower arrangement yourself," Mist noted as she entered the small shop. "All you need is a touch of red, perhaps some berries above one ear."

"I know!" Maisie said. "These last-minute orders are crazy this year. I'm not complaining though. It's delightful to put them together. You know that already, which is why you order individual stems and greenery."

"True," Mist said, surveying the lush assortment Maisie had available to work with. "And so many roses," she added, spying three tubs filled with the rich red blooms.

"Well, you can't go wrong with roses," Maisie said lightly. "Especially red during the holiday season."

Mist eyed a set of tiny vases, each with a sprig of holly, a red carnation, and a touch of baby's breath. "How lovely. For a special occasion?"

Maisie nodded. "They're for Millie. She wanted something small to give each of the volunteers who help with the library's literacy program."

"A wonderful idea," Mist said. "And a lovely way to thank the volunteers who help."

"I thought so," Maisie agreed. "I made an extra, hoping she'll keep one for herself. I'm going to encourage her to. She does so much for others, running that library with little funding and few helpers."

Mist nodded in agreement, knowing Millie's dedication to the library was heartfelt, a gift to the community.

"Oh!" Maisie raised one finger in the air as if just remembering an important detail. "I have something for you." She hurried into the little shop's back room and returned with a cardboard box, which she tilted forward for Mist to see. "I received these by accident with one of the flower orders, and the company told me to keep them rather than send them back. I thought you might have a use for them."

Mist reached into the box and lifted out a perfectly formed pine cone. Smiling, she placed it back inside the box and pulled out another, this one smaller. "Isn't nature amazing? The wonders it can create! It's truly the master artist of all."

"You know I agree," Maisie said. "It's part of the reason running this shop is so delightful." She clipped the end of a white lily's stem and inserted it into an arrangement. "Speaking of artists, your miniature paintings are all the rage again for Christmas gifts, like every year. Especially that new one, the fox in the snow. A woman came by who bought four of them, all the same. She wanted six, but that was all Clive's gallery had. She left her contact information there."

This comment brought a smile to Mist's face, not only because her new design was well received but because Maisie had made a point of saying the woman could be reached. Mist always had a small back stock prepared, especially around the holidays, and Maisie knew it. As it happened, she did have two more of that particular miniature painting back in her room at the hotel.

"I'll drop two more off later today."

"How did I know that already?" Maisie grinned as she snipped another lily stem.

"You simply have an amazing sense of the unknown." Mist smiled, thanked Maisie for the pine cones, and headed back to the hotel.

SEVEN

Hollister, the formerly homeless man who now lived in the spare room—technically a storage room but conveniently fixed up to encourage him inside—opened the door shortly after Mist, standing outside and, in a rare assertive movement, thunked her heel forcefully on the weathered hallway floor. Knocking on the door served no purpose, since the man could not hear. But the vibration of the old hotel's wooden floorboards sufficed to alert him to Mist's presence. It was a code they had developed in order for Mist to be able to enter the room without disturbing his privacy. This allowed her to use the refrigerator in the room, both to store prepped food for the kitchen and café and to leave Hollister meals.

An exceptionally reclusive man, it was rare that Hollister would come into the hotel, much less mingle with others. Still, on special occasions, Mist had an uncanny way of coaxing him out. And there seemed no more special occasion that having Stephen and Erika in the front parlor, conversing by sign language in front the fireplace.

It had come to Mist's attention over the years that Hollister had a particular weakness for hot cocoa. She'd developed the skill of holding a hot cup of the beverage steady while deploying the heel-to-floor announcement of her arrival. It was a combined movement that delighted her, so much so that she'd occasionally practice it in the kitchen just for fun.

Hollister greeted Mist with a nod of his head, and his eyes grew wide as he spied the mug of hot cocoa in one hand. With the other hand, she motioned for him to follow her. When he hesitated, she raised the mug of hot cocoa closer to her face and breathed in the chocolatey scent, closing her eyes to indicate its appeal. To her delight, the bribery worked, and he followed her to the living room, taking a tentative seat across from Stephen and Erika.

It was no surprise that Erika, having been clued in by Mist earlier about Hollister's disability, raised her hands and signed *hello*. Yet it was an enormous surprise, to Mist especially, when Hollister did the same in return. Her face must have shown her amazement because Hollister shrugged his shoulders and smiled as if he'd just pulled off a marvelous feat which, in fact, he had. He turned back to Erika and Steven and signed something slightly longer. Both Steven and Erika laughed, and Erika translated Hollister's message for Mist. *You never asked.*

Mist lowered herself into a chair, half to steady her legs and half to join the conversation. She addressed Erika. "Could you teach me? Just a few phrases?"

"Of course," Erika said. "What would you like to start with?"

"I… I'm not sure," Mist said, taking a moment to think. "How about *hello*?"

Erika motioned the greeting, and Mist copied her movement.

"Now say hello to your friend," Erika suggested.

Mist turned to Hollister and signed the greeting. When Hollister repeated it back to her, Mist felt her eyes fill with tears. She turned back to Erika. "This is amazing!"

"Now you have a new tool." Stephen signed, and Erika translated verbally.

"A wonderful tool," Mist said. "And I'd love to learn more. How about one additional phrase right now? Could you ask Hollister what he would like me to learn to say?"

Erika signed the question, and Hollister replied, instigating a round of laughter between all but Mist, who had yet to learn the new phrase.

Slowly Erika taught Mist a sequence of movements as both Steven and Hollister looked on, smiling first and then laughing as Mist became more adept at the hand motions.

"Now you have two phrases," Erika said.

"Wonderful," Mist said. "But perhaps I should know what it means?"

"Of course," Erika said with a grin. "It means would you like some hot cocoa?"

Mist gave Hollister a mischievous look. "Well, I see we've covered the most important phrases." She looked back at Erika. "Thank you. I know you teach all year, so you deserve to relax during the holiday. But I'm so grateful."

"I'll teach you more before we leave," Erika said with a liveliness she hadn't shown before the exchange. "That way you won't have to make hot cocoa around the clock." She translated that into sign language, and Steven and Hollister both smiled.

"That's a perfect plan," Mist said. "And now I'll leave you all to visit with each other while I attend to culinary tasks. Thank you, Erika."

"Thank *you*, Mist. You've reminded me why I went into this profession to begin with. Communication opens so many doors."

To Mist's delight, Hollister remained in the front parlor as she headed for the kitchen.

"How on earth did we not know that Hollister knew sign language?" Betty said as Mist filled her in on the exchange. "My, my, my." She pulled a caramel from her apron pocket, disposed of the wrapper, and popped it into her mouth.

"We never had occasion to find out," Mist said as she began to chop fresh dill for dinner rolls. "This is the first time we've had a hearing-impaired guest stay with us. And we've always allowed Hollister distance, letting him make the choice to approach us when he felt ready."

"What a gift this is for all of us," Betty mused. "'Tis the season!"

"Yes, the season of miracles both large and small." Mist lifted her arm over a glazed pottery bowl of warm water, yeast, and a variety of other ingredients, letting the chopped herbs fall through the air as if sprinkling fairy dust.

Betty moved to the kitchen window and looked outside, sighing. "We could use a miracle with the weather about now. I'd love to see our guests get to take a walk or play in the snow without the wind blowing them sideways. Have you heard the forecast? I don't see the storm letting up."

Mist smiled. "You know I pay more attention to the *nowcast* than the forecast." She knew Betty would understand her reasoning, knowing Mist believed time to be relative. And in that sense, it was always *now*.

"Yes, I do know that," Betty said. "But I was hoping it might clear by tomorrow night, Christmas Eve."

"Perhaps it will clear for Christmas Day instead," Mist suggested. "Then everyone could enjoy outdoor winter activities. There's more to do in the daylight, and the temperatures would be better."

"You're right about all that. I was just hoping… Well, it's not important." Betty looked away as Mist gave her a curious look. "Storm or not, the guests will have a wonderful holiday."

"We'll make sure they will." Adding flour to the bowl, Mist blended the ingredients for the dinner rolls together. After lightly kneading the dough, she set it aside under a warm cloth.

"Oh, I almost forgot to tell you," Betty said. "Clive was looking for you."

Mist nodded. "I have a feeling I know why. Maisie mentioned he might need two more fox paintings for a customer." She pointed to a small package she'd prepared and set by the door. "I'll run them down to the gallery while the rolls rise."

"Should I watch them?"

Although she knew what Betty meant, Mist had the sudden image of Betty hovering over the rolls without so much as blinking. She fought back a giggle, which resulted in an amusing sound not unlike a hiccup.

"I just pictured you staring at the rolls as if to keep them from running away."

"You're saying that's not necessary?"

"If a watched pot never boils..." Mist let the sentence trail off as she donned a heavy jacket and wrapped a thick wool scarf around her head and neck.

"Then watched rolls never rise." Betty laughed. "You go on down to Clive's place. I'll watch the rolls and anything else that needs supervision around here."

"Thanks, Betty." Mist, package in hand, opened the kitchen's side door to a rush of wind and snow. She stepped outside, closed the door quickly, and headed to the gallery.

EIGHT

The warmth of the gallery was a welcome relief as Mist stepped inside. Even the short walk, not quite two blocks, had been enough for a chill to invade her jacket and a cold sting to settle across her face.

Clive caught sight of her as she entered. Occupied with a customer at a jewelry counter, he waved her toward the back. She meandered in that direction, taking note of the activity around her, pleased to see his business doing well.

With two days remaining before Christmas, it wasn't a surprise to see the gallery crowded. The general tendency toward last-minute shopping always guaranteed a rush right before the holiday. Still, it was remarkably busy throughout the artsy shop, both around the jewelry displays and along the walls of artwork. And remarkably colorful as well, the artsy space accentuated by the bright knit caps and scarves that accompanied the winter outerwear of customers throughout.

Mist placed the wrapped fox paintings on Clive's desk in the back and returned to the shop area, enjoying the lively scene. Holiday music serenaded shoppers, and she smiled to hear the "Little Drummer

Boy" playing overhead. The aroma of hot cider added another touch to the ambiance. Mist was pleased Clive had agreed with her suggestion to add music and beverages this year. It not only created more of a festive atmosphere, but it encouraged customers to linger. Perhaps they'd shop more, or they'd happen upon a friend, or they'd simply enjoy the charm of a small-town gallery. Either way, both the business and customers came out ahead.

Spotting Clara and Andrew, Mist headed in that direction, meeting up with them in front of a Christmas tree displaying silver ornaments. The popular item, created and handmade by Clive, featured a tiny Yogo sapphire set in a traditional holiday design. Whether a tree, a star, a snowman, a wreath, or another seasonal motif, each ornament was stunning, a perfect gift or remembrance of time spent in Montana's sapphire country. What had started as a special Christmas gift from Clive to Betty one year had now become one of the gallery's best-selling items, thanks to Betty encouraging Clive that such a sweet design idea needed to be enjoyed by others, not just herself.

"Mist!" Clara exclaimed. "How nice to see you out and about! We were just looking at these ornaments. I remember when Clive gave Betty the first one." She turned to Andrew. "She was so surprised."

"We'll definitely choose one to take home with us," Andrew said. "We just can't decide which one."

"He really wishes there was one with a toy train," Clara whispered to Mist. "It was his favorite Christmas gift as a child."

"It's true," Andrew said. "It was what I wanted more than anything in the world at the time. I think I was about six years old."

"And did you get one?" Mist asked.

"Indeed, I did. And it was as marvelous as I thought it would be—a bright red engine with black trim, a tall smokestack, a tiny bell hanging from the roof, and a silver cowcatcher."

"A cowcatcher?" Clara looked at Andrew, puzzled.

"It's called a pilot now," he explained. "It's the grate on the front of an engine, made to help clear obstacles off the track."

"Oh yes." Clara nodded her head. "Now I know what you mean."

"Do you still have the train?" Mist asked, enchanted by the description.

Andrew shook his head but smiled. "No. That was so many decades ago. We moved, and things got lost, others given away."

"But you still have the memory."

Andrew's face beamed. "Yes, I do, and I'm delighted to think of it now."

Mist turned to Clara. "Did you also have a favorite toy?"

"Oh yes! And I think you'd be surprised by what it was." Clara looked from Mist to Andrew and back again, her statement clearly a challenge.

"A doll," Andrew guessed. Clara shook her head.

"A book," Mist suggested, having always loved receiving books as a child.

Again, Clara shook her head. "Wrong and wrong," she said, clearly delighted with their incorrect guesses. "It was a science kit!"

"Really, how interesting," Andrew exclaimed.

"It was wonderful." Clara's face lit up as she described the microscope, slides, petri dish, and more included in the kit. "I would conduct experiments and pretend I was discovering the secrets of the universe through that microscope's lens."

"My brilliant scientist!" Andrew wrapped his arm around Clara's waist.

"What a wonderful gift for a child," Mist mused. "There's so much we can see through a microscope, as well as others that can only be seen from a distance." She then looked at the tree with Clive's ornaments. "I'll let you two work on your decision here. Maybe choose one to get now and then next year come back and choose another."

"That's a wonderful idea!" Clara exclaimed. "That way, we don't need to decide on only one; we're simply deciding which to get first."

"Exactly," Mist said. "And you have something to look forward to in the future."

Leaving Clara and Andrew to the task at hand, Mist circled the room, taking in the festive atmosphere. A young couple admired a Western landscape by another local artist and discussed where it might fit in their home. A thirtysomething man, shopping by himself, debated between two sapphire pendants. And Daniel Hutton stood quietly by the hot cider, observing the joyful crowd yet keeping apart.

"Quite the crowd, don't you think?" Mist said as she approached.

"Yes," Daniel said. "And they all look so... full of life. Enjoying the world around them, carefree." He took a sip of hot cider and fell quiet.

"It does seem that way," Mist said, glancing around the gallery. "But I would say these are simply carefree moments you're seeing, and no one has carefree moments all the time."

Daniel seemed to contemplate Mist's words but remained silent, and Mist sensed the time to merely observe the room was what he needed. In any case, a batch of dinner rolls called, as well as other fare for the café's evening meal. She said as much, excusing herself to take care of needed preparations.

Clive caught her at the door, having finished with his customer. "Thanks for dropping off the paintings. I called the woman who asked for them, and she was thrilled. She'll come by tomorrow morning to pick them up. These are the last gifts she needed."

"That's wonderful," Mist said.

"It's amazing that you had just what she wanted." Clive noticed a man waiting to speak with him at the jewelry counter and signaled that he'd be right there.

"Just a coincidence, I suppose." Mist said lightly.

"You're awfully good with coincidences, Mist. I'd better help this customer. Thank you." Clive stepped away, then turned back. "I'll see you at dinner."

Mist laughed. If there was one thing everyone could count on, it was that Clive would never miss a meal. "Of course you will."

Walking back to the hotel, she smiled as she leaned forward into the wind. A *coincidence* she had said. A *mystery*. Yes, the secret stash of mini paintings and prepared canvases was a mystery indeed. A very carefully planned mystery that she purposely built up all year for just these occasions. Which made her wonder whether coincidences could be created, a thought she pondered all the way back to the hotel.

NINE

Mist leaned against the archway that separated the hotel foyer from the front parlor and watched Michael, asleep by the fireplace, head resting against the back of his favorite chair. A book lay open in his lap as if he'd lowered it unknowingly as sleep swept over him, not allowing enough warning for him to set it aside. The glow of the fire's light on his face looked peaceful and comforting, yet she sensed unrest below the surface. It wasn't something she could describe. It was simply a feeling that something wasn't quite right.

"Still worried about Michael?" Betty said quietly.

Deep in thought, Mist hadn't heard Betty approach. She turned toward the hotelkeeper and smiled. "A little."

Betty rubbed Mist's back in a motherly fashion. "I imagine he's just catching up on rest. I heard him talking to Clive, and it sounded like getting that outreach program set up has been a lot of work."

"It has been," Mist admitted. "He's been preoccupied with it for weeks, establishing the curriculum for the courses, assigning student teachers to the classes he would normally be teaching next semester, preparing to move down to faculty housing closer to here…"

Her voice trailed off, unconvinced despite the logical explanation. "Of course that makes my heart sing, the thought of him being closer. I just wonder where it will be. He says it hasn't been officially assigned yet."

"Well, wherever it ends up being, it's bound to be more convenient," Betty said. "Driving back and forth between here and Missoula to visit each other hasn't been easy for you two, not with his teaching schedule at the university there and your work here at the hotel."

Mist smiled. "This is hardly work. It's more like a delightful adventure every day. Cooking, decorating, and helping guests enjoy their visit. How could anyone possibly call that work?"

"Some people would," Betty pointed out. "I'm sure some people do."

"Then I hope they find something else, something to fill their soul with joy."

"Not everyone is able to do that," Betty mused.

Mist contemplated the statement. For all she spoke of joy and light and inspiration, she was not oblivious to reality. "I know that," she said quietly. "For them, I hope for five minutes each day of peace, a short respite from work that is a burden, from the grief of loss, from that which brings them stress or sadness."

"A short walk, maybe," Betty suggested. "Or a few minutes lost in a book, or a phone call to a friend. But what if they can't even do that?"

Mist inhaled and exhaled, feeling the air fill her lungs and depart. "Then they breathe. Sometimes it's the only option." As she spoke, a sense of gratitude washed over her. She lived in a wonderful town, surrounded by caring friends, free to follow her passions of painting and cooking. In addition, she had the pleasure of meeting and interacting with intriguing guests, each with a different story. It was a charmed existence, and she was thankful for it every day.

"I'd better refill those glazed cinnamon nuts again," Betty said, motioning to the lobby counter where the bowl sat, half-empty.

"Yes, I suppose you should." Mist laughed. "Most of the guests and half the town count on that bowl staying full. I'll see how everyone is doing out there."

Mist stepped into the front parlor as Betty retreated to the kitchen. She found Nora in a seat near the front window, admiring the old-fashioned decorations on the hotel's Christmas tree. The tall Douglas fir could almost be called a living history, bearing handmade art by local schoolchildren, some now grown, along with ornaments dating back to Betty's childhood as well as others contributed by guests over the years. To add to this, the collection of silver ornaments that Clive crafted for Betty each year continued to grow, each one different.

"A lovely tree," Nora said as Mist approached. Stephen and Erika soon joined them, both agreeing as indicated through a combination of speech and sign language.

"Those silver ornaments are especially wonderful," Erika said, reaching out to touch a dangling snowman. "They're so unique."

"Have you seen the ones for sale at Clive's gallery?" Mist said. "He designs and handcrafts them himself."

"I'll have to check those out," Nora said. "Maybe Whitney and I could choose one to take home with us."

"That's what we did," Clara said, joining the conversation. "We decided on a wreath ornament this time." She turned to Mist and smiled. "Since we couldn't find a train or a microscope."

Seeing puzzled looks on the others, Mist explained, "We were discussing favorite toys from childhood earlier."

"Yes," Clara said. "The train for Andrew, the microscope for me."

Nora nodded. "Wouldn't it be something to have a tree full of ornaments representing favorite toys? Mine would have to be a teddy bear with golden fur and a red ribbon around his neck. How I loved that bear!"

"That's how I felt about a tiny china horse I had." Erika brought her right thumb and index finger close together, indicating a height of just over an inch. "It was so delicate, and I was always afraid I'd break it."

"Did you?" Stephen signed.

Erika shook her head. "No. I was very careful. I kept it in a glass case and didn't play with it. I even displayed it on a small mirror so I could pretend I had two."

Again, Stephen signed, and Erika translated. "I wish I had been that careful. I had a model plane that I worked hard to build. Even painted it blue with a lightning bolt on the side. It only took one clumsy step to crush it one day when it was on the floor."

Whitney entered while the discussion was in progress but maneuvered her crutches across the room to one of Mist's paintings, hanging toward the back of the parlor. She shuffled her crutches to one side and raised her free arm. Without touching the painting's surface, she traced the outline of one of the trees, as if analyzing the shape of the branches. Mist excused herself from the conversation by the tree and crossed over to stand next to the girl.

"Do you like the painting?" Mist asked, sensing a direct but casual approach would be best to reach the quiet girl.

Whitney jumped as Mist spoke, and her arm fell to her side.

"Sorry," Mist said. "I didn't mean to startle you. I saw you observing the painting and was curious what you thought of it." She shifted her weight from one leg to the other, taking an observation stance that one might take if looking at a painting for the first time. "I rather like the trees in that one." Of course she liked the trees, which was why she'd painted them as she did.

"I love the trees," Whitney said, turning back to look at them again. "The branches seem so real to me, like I could climb them or something."

Mist nodded. "I can see that. How high do you think you could climb?" Neither Mist nor Whitney made note of the fact that, armed with crutches, she wouldn't be climbing trees at all in the near future. But that didn't matter. The discussion wasn't about climbing trees at all; it was simply about the painting itself.

"Probably up to here," Whitney said, indicating a branch about a third of the way up the tree.

"Why to there?"

"Because the branches aren't as sturdy above that one," Whitney explained. "You can tell from the way the lines are." She turned to face Mist. "Do you live here?"

"I do," Mist said. "I live in a little room behind the kitchen. That's where I paint too."

"I know you painted this."

"How did you know that?"

"The man with the funny accent told me."

"I see." Mist smiled. "I imagine you mean the professor. He's from England, so his speech sounds a little different from ours."

"I think it sounds cool," Whitney said.

"I do too," Mist said. "I also think the way you see those branches in the painting is cool."

"Thanks," Whitney said. "I love to draw and paint. I just don't have time with all the team practices. I mean, I haven't had time. But now..." She glanced at her ankle.

"I see," Mist said, looking down at the injured leg as if just now noticing it although she'd paid attention to it since the girl first arrived. "You'll have to stay off that for a while, won't you?"

Whitney nodded and lowered her voice. "Yeah. My mom is disappointed."

"I see." Mist found this intriguing, that Whitney would mention her mom's feelings rather than her own. "And how about you? Are you disappointed too?"

Whitney shrugged. "I guess."

"Well, maybe it's a chance to do something different, like drawing and painting," Mist suggested. "What do you think?"

Again, Whitney shrugged, but it was a smaller shrug. "Maybe."

Mist stood back, as if inspecting the painting again. "There are all kinds of possibilities within that *maybe*."

"Like what?"

"That's up to you," Mist said. "After all, it's your *maybe*. You get to do what you want with it."

TEN

The day before Christmas was always filled with activity. Mist rose even earlier than usual in order to tend to artwork and still get a head start on dinner preparations. The Christmas Eve feast was arguably the highlight of the Timberton Hotel's holiday season. They'd managed to keep to just one seating this year by rearranging tables to accommodate a few extra parties. All the hotel guests would join in along with many of the townsfolk. A few more would travel into town for the occasion, having made reservations early enough.

Much to Mist's amusement, Betty waltzed into the kitchen soon after she did, humming a Christmas carol and smiling at no one in particular. Pleased to see the hotelkeeper in light spirits, she was still puzzled by the unusual behavior. Not that Betty wasn't cheerful most days; she was. But this level of enthusiasm was peculiar.

"Dare I ask what has brought on this mood?" Mist glanced at Betty with curiosity as she filled a kettle with water and put it on the stove to boil.

"Haven't you looked outside?"

To her surprise, Mist realized she hadn't. She'd been focused on preparing the gifts she planned to give to guests, setting up small canvases on a special easel that held a half dozen at a time. This allowed her to paint backgrounds in advance, preparing all but a singular image to be added the night before giving them away. She never knew what those images would be when she began. The inspiration for each always hit her at some point between the arrival of guests and Christmas morning.

"No, I guess I haven't," Mist admitted. She moved to the kitchen window and looked out. The snow had stopped falling, and the wind had died down to just a breeze. In addition, the sky was a lighter gray. "How wonderful," she said, turning back to Betty. "It looks like the clouds might even clear."

"Yes, it's fantastic!" Betty chirped.

"Betty…," Mist said softly with a smile. "How much coffee have you had today?" She suspected coffee, which she often endearingly called Java Love, might be the cause of Betty's effervescence.

"The usual," Betty said. "A cup early in the morning and one more when Clive stopped by to visit—and check for baked goods, naturally. Why?"

"No reason," Mist said lightly. She checked the progress of the kettle's water and found it starting to boil. She fixed herself a cup of peppermint tea and then pulled out various fixings from the refrigerator and set to making a simple breakfast for hotel guests only.

Christmas Eve was the one day of the year that local townsfolk were invited to dinner only, rather than breakfast and dinner. This allowed a quick morning meal and cleanup, leaving time for preparing the more extravagant dinner. No one in town minded the café being closed that morning; they all knew the evening meal would be a feast.

Hotel guests, appetites satisfied after a casual breakfast of steel-cut oats with brown sugar, honeydew melon slices, and a dish that Mist simply called a holiday scramble—potatoes, mushrooms, and any variety of other things she fancied that particular morning—sauntered off to various activities. A cozy fire and soft instrumental Christmas music created a warm ambiance in the front parlor where most chose to spend the rest of the morning.

Much to the delight of several guests, Mist had set up an "artist's buffet," a last-minute inspiration for an indoor Christmas Eve day. A wooden table, usually set against the back wall of the front parlor, now sat several feet into the room, chairs set around it. The center boasted boxes, crates, and baskets filled with potential purveyors of inspiration: squares of heavy paper, die-cut wooden shapes, watercolor paint and chalky pastels, satin ribbons and old buttons from Mist's favorite closet, silk thread and beads, rubber stamps and ink pads, the pine cones that Maisie had given her, felt, glue, scissors, and a variety of other supplies.

Just as she'd hoped, the enticing assortment of colors, textures, and shapes did not go unnoticed. The table seemed to have a magnetic appeal, even without announcing its existence. Within minutes of the early meal ending, several chairs were occupied.

Erika, Nora, and a less sullen than usual Whitney were absorbed in choosing materials to work with. Erika held a square-shaped piece of wood and was choosing items to make a collage. Nora sorted beads, deciding which to string in what order on a green silk thread, a necklace in the making. And Whitney, who had found a charcoal pencil, a sheet of sketch paper, and the watercolor paints, stared at the blank paper with focused concentration, pencil hovering, ready to use.

Andrew and the professor settled into a game of chess, Michael and Clive excused themselves to check on the gallery, as well as something to do with Clive's construction project. Mist, a firm believer in free will, had quietly watched them go, not feeling it her—or anyone's—right to suggest that the day before Christmas might be better spent relaxing.

Steven sat by the fireplace, having selected an anthology of science fiction stories from a bookcase the hotel kept stocked with a wide variety of reading material.

Daniel Hutton stood by the front window, looking out while half-engaged in conversation with Clara. Every few minutes, he'd touch an ornament on the Christmas tree, nod in response to something Clara had said, and then return to observing the world outside. Periodically, he'd check his phone and put it away again.

"It seems the guests are content," Betty said, joining Mist. "For the most part."

"Yes, for the most part." Mist eyed Daniel Hutton, pleased to see him responding somewhat to Clara.

Whatever was troubling him—she felt sure something was—Clara was an easy person to open up to. She was kind, calm, and never pushy. If a person needed a safe haven for thoughts, she was the ultimate caring listener.

"And the kitchen is clear whenever you need it," Betty said. "Maisie popped in the side door a little while ago and helped with the dishes."

"How kind of her. I don't know how she does it, running her florist business, raising Clay Jr., and still helping here all the time. I'm glad she has Clayton to help when he's not attending to fire station responsibilities."

"I think the time she spends at the hotel gives her a break from those other areas of her life," Betty suggested. "Even if it's only for ten minutes when she stops by."

"I can see that," Mist agreed. "I also know she's sincerely trying to make things easier for us. It's wonderful." She glanced around at the various activities in progress and excused herself to check on the crafts buffet. Hearing an ongoing conversation as she approached, she chose to remain quiet and straighten the supplies.

"I understand," Nora said to Erika. "I felt that way about my last job. I was burned out, and it affected not only my work but also my emotions."

Erika nodded as she glued a shiny gold button on her collage in progress. "That's how I've felt lately. I've always loved teaching, but it seemed like the joy was gone. I've been thinking about retiring early, which I never thought I would. But then today I felt inspired again." She looked up at Mist. "Thank you, and thank your friend, Hollister."

"If you teach me how to say 'thank you.'"

"I'll be happy to do that," Erika said.

Nora added a red bead to a multicolored group already strung. She contemplated a bowl of beads, deciding which to add next.

Mist noticed a pattern to the beads Nora was choosing, dark, then light, then dark, then light, but in differing colors. The contrast was pleasing, and she pondered what it would look like when it was finished. Would she continue the same pattern? Would she vary it along the way? Would she add a statement piece—there were quite a few charms and larger beads to choose from—in the middle?

"What do you think?" Nora asked suddenly, as if she'd read Mist's thoughts. She held the partial necklace up in the air.

"I think you have a lot of choices." Mist lifted the bowl of beads, which she had gathered little by little during the year. "Choices are a nice thing to have." She shook the bowl gently, watching the beads roll around, and then set it back on the table. "I'd go with whichever strikes your fancy at the moment. Or simply close your eyes, reach in, and pick one." She did exactly that, pulling out a brilliant purple bead with a meandering green stripe around the middle.

Seemingly satisfied with the directions—not that they were directions at all, really—Nora returned to the task as well as to the discussion with Erika.

Daniel Hutton now stood by the fireplace, alone, a snifter of brandy in his hand. He remained quiet, although he'd stopped looking at his phone. Mist took the opportunity to engage the doctor in conversation.

"Dr. Hutton, are you enjoying your stay?" Mist said lightly. "May I get you anything?"

"Just call me Daniel. I'm trying to leave the medical world behind on this trip."

"Is that working?" Mist, already suspecting the answer, was not surprised to hear him say he was finding it difficult to distance himself from current cases in the office.

"Christmas is a tough time of year for many patients and families," Daniel said. "Especially those waiting for test results."

"I can imagine." Mist left her comment at that, not wishing to push. If Daniel wanted to share more of his thoughts, he would. And if he didn't, perhaps he was getting his wish for a temporary reprieve. When he took a sip of brandy and remained quiet, she excused herself and moved on.

Circling back to the crafts table, Mist was pleased to see Whitney had sketched an old barn surrounded by trees of differing heights. "Lovely," she said.

"You think so?" Whitney looked up, pleased.

"I do," Mist said. "I love that you've made some of the trees taller than others."

"I want to paint them, the barn too. But not, like, heavy paint." Whitney regarded the sketch as if imagining it with color.

"Watercolors might give you the look you want." Mist retrieved a set of watercolors from the craft selections and set it beside Whitney. "Try it. Experiment."

"What if I don't like it?"

Mist smiled. "There's more paper."

Whitney smiled back, and with that, Mist left the crafters to their decisions and moved on to the kitchen to make some of her own.

ELEVEN

Shortly after noon, Mist placed a large platter of assorted cheeses, fresh fruit, and a variety of crackers in the front parlor to appease midday appetites. The light fare would be enough to tide everyone over until the veritable feast of Christmas Eve dinner that evening. Those guests who had remained indoors helped themselves to the light offerings. Others, seeing the snow had stopped and the wind had settled, had already ventured out for short walks or to browse shops still open for last-minute shoppers.

Clara and Andrew lingered by the fireplace, which Clive had stoked before heading to the gallery. Nora and Whitney returned to the craft table, continuing their projects from earlier.

Daniel had checked his phone after breakfast and then taken off for a short country drive on his own. Stephen and Erika went shopping for souvenir gifts to take home to family members. And Michael, per his usual mode this holiday season, was off helping Clive, taking the professor with him this time.

"It feels like a busier holiday than others," Mist said to Betty, who sat at the kitchen's center island with a mug of coffee, watching Mist pull ingredients, spices, condiments, pots, pans, and any number of

other things from various spots around the room.
B09GKGYPL9

"Maybe because people have been inside during the storm," Betty suggested. She took a sip of coffee and then set the cup down. "All that indoor activity makes it seem busier than it is. Every Christmas is busy here between hotel guests and café meals. But guests usually saunter in and out during the day when the weather is nicer."

"That's true," Mist said as she rinsed fresh greens, dividing them between two large salad bowls. To one, she added chopped apples and pecans. To the other, apples only, an option for anyone with a nut allergy. Small signs in festive calligraphy would announce the difference once the salads were on the buffet.

"What can I do to help?" Betty stood and took her empty coffee cup to the sink. Both she and Mist turned to the kitchen door as another voice joined in.

"Could I help too? I'm feeling restless." Clara stood halfway in and halfway out, her fingers drumming on the door.

"I don't see why not," Betty quipped. "You're family after all these years."

"That's how I feel," Clara said. "Coming here for Christmas feels like coming home. I look forward to it all year."

"That's exactly what we hope for," Mist said, smiling. "And if food prep makes you feel even more at home, you're welcome to it." She pointed to two bowls, one with sweet potatoes, the other with green beans. Two large roasting pans sat nearby along with an appropriate knife.

"I can do some of those," Betty said, fetching another knife from a wood block on a side counter. She joined Clara, and the two set to work.

"Thanks for spending some time with Dr. Hutton by the Christmas tree earlier," Mist said. "You're always so good at drawing people out. I hope he's enjoying his stay. Oh, do you think you might be able to find out what his favorite toy was as a child? Like the train was for Andrew and the microscope for you?"

"I think I can do that," Clara said. "It could be a conversation starter."

"Yes," Betty chimed in. "He's been so quiet. Is there something he needs? Something we could do to help him enjoy his stay more?"

Clara shook her head. "No, he doesn't need anything. He's just…" Her voice trailed off, and she seemed to choose her words carefully. "He's just worried about a particular patient and hoping for news."

"He sounds dedicated and very caring," Mist said. "Two wonderful traits in a doctor. What is his field? Do you know?"

Clara set a potato on a cutting board and sliced it in two. "Oncology."

"Ah, that's a tough specialty," Betty said, shaking her head. "It must be difficult, having to deliver bad news sometimes."

"Or delightful to deliver good news," Mist pointed out, always looking to see both sides of a situation.

She watched Clara, who continued to cut the sweet potatoes into a reasonable serving size. "Then again, it would be frustrating to have no news."

"Oh yes," Betty said. "To have to wait, not knowing test results, for example. That happened to a friend of mine. For two weeks, she felt like her future was being held hostage. It almost drove her crazy, running all the possibilities through her mind."

"Exactly," Clara said. "I think that would be especially hard during the holidays." She placed the cut pieces of potato in the roasting pan and began to cut another.

"It's a shame he can't get his mind off it, just for a few days, to enjoy the season," Betty said. "He must be close to this patient."

"Yes," Clara said, not looking up. "He is."

Mist nodded as she covered the salads and set them aside, ready to place in the spare refrigerator. "Then I hope he gets whatever news he's hoping for. Peace of mind would be a wonderful gift at Christmas. Or any time of the year, for that matter." She took a lemon from a wire basket of citrus fruit, washed it, and began to grate zest into a small pottery dish.

"What's Andrew up to this afternoon?" Betty asked.

"He went down to meet Clive and Michael at the gallery," Clara said. "They needed some sort of help with a project."

"Probably the renovation over at the old building where Mist's café used to be," Betty said.

"You're not moving the Moonglow Café out of the hotel, are you?" Clara said, alarmed.

Mist almost laughed. "Don't worry. The café isn't going anywhere. The Timberton Hotel is its home now. Clive is just pushing to get new tenants into that building the first of the year."

"What a relief," Clara said. "One of the things I love most about staying here is enjoying those lovely aromas that float out of this kitchen and around the hotel."

"You'll have plenty of those today," Mist said, delighted at the reminder that food could please more than one sense. "The sweet potatoes will be roasted with vanilla, the brisket, braised with red wine, and the green beans cooked with lemon zest."

"And that's not counting dessert," Betty added.

"True," Mist said. "Add caramel to the list."

"Vanilla, lemon, wine, caramel…," Clara listed. "I can hardly wait!"

Mist smiled again. Christmas Eve dinner was always worth waiting for. But like all good things, anticipation was half the joy.

TWELVE

True to her own personal tradition, Mist stood quietly in the café before opening it up for dinner. This time was precious to her, a peaceful prelude to a festive evening that would be filled with laughter and conversation. Here, alone, she could wander through the room, checking that the flower arrangements on each table were placed in such a way as to please guests yet allow conversation. She could make sure the buffet was set just so, that the tiny lights along the ceiling were twinkling, that soft Christmas music was flowing at a pleasant volume. In short, she could look around the room and then close her eyes to let the ambiance sink in. When it did, she'd open her eyes again, walk to the doors, and open them.

Something felt different about this year, and she couldn't quite put her finger on it. The guests were all lovely, as always. The townsfolk were all supportive of anything at the hotel. Michael, even though preoccupied with changes in his life, was his usual sweet and kind self. There wasn't anything in particular that was different about this year's season. Yet it felt like a change was in the air.

She had dressed more formally than in the past yet still in keeping with her personal bohemian style. It was an idea she'd pondered after seeing a remarkable dress—forest-green silk with a high neckline and full, swirling skirt—come into Second Hand Sally's. Betty had convinced her to make the purchase, assuring her that Christmas Eve was a perfect time to wear something special. Of course, Mist had added her own touches: an asymmetrical necklace of African turquoise and crystal, a wide copper arm cuff, and dangling earrings of tiny Czech seed beads. She'd clipped her hair up into a loose bun, held by a vintage silver hair clip. The fact that none of the jewelry matched each other delighted her to no end.

She opened the doors that separated the café from the front entryway, and an enthusiastic crowd began to flow into the room. Clara and Andrew had dressed for the evening, Clara in a soft red sweater and skirt set accessorized with a string of pearls, Andrew in a suit. Steven and Erika had also donned evening wear. Although first-timers, they had anticipated an upscale meal based on the email exchange when they'd made reservations. The professor entered in slacks and an argyle sweater, which seemed to fit his personality perfectly.

Daniel Hutton, on a phone call across the lobby, ended the call and took a deep breath. Mist could almost see the tension he'd been carrying melt away as he exhaled. To her delight, he chose to sit with the professor, Clara, and Andrew, clearly open to the social aspect of the meal. Michael took a seat at that table as well. Nora and Whitney completed the attendance of overnight guests. Whitney's crutches, decorated with ribbons from the earlier craft table, added to the festive decor.

Cheerful townsfolk and visitors completed the crowd. Maisie, with a seat saved next to Clayton and Clay Jr., took to filling crystal glasses with chilled water as Mist and Betty brought out whatever hot dishes couldn't be set out beforehand. In no time, the hungry crowd lined up at the buffet and began loading plates with wine-braised brisket, mushroom-and-cashew wellington, mixed greens with apples, pecans, and champagne vinaigrette, hazelnut green beans with lemon zest, vanilla-roasted sweet potatoes, and rosemary butter rolls.

Clive made the rounds, offering wine and other beverages as well as holiday-themed jokes that set the room laughing. *How much does it cost Santa to park his sleigh and reindeer? Nothing, it's on the house! Which of Santa's reindeer has the cleanest antlers? Comet!* And the professor's favorite: *What did the English teacher call Santa's helpers? Subordinate Clauses!*

Lively jazz music flowed from overhead speakers hidden behind twinkling lights, moving from "Winter Wonderland" to "Jingle Bell Rock" to "Holly Jolly Christmas" to "Feliz Navidad." The music, conversation, laughter, and enticing aromas of the holiday meal created an atmosphere bursting with joy. Each tiny sound—a fork tapping a plate, the kitchen door swinging open as the buffet was continually restocked, a chair scraping against the floor as a guest stood to retrieve a second helping—only served to add welcome percussion to the festive arrangement of sensations.

"Delicious as always!" William "Wild Bill" Guthrie proclaimed.

"So true!" Clayton said. He looked over at Maisie, who had joined her family at Mist and Betty's insistence once all the water glasses had been filled.

By the time dessert was served—a decadent sticky toffee pudding topped with a choice of whipped cream, vanilla ice cream, or both—the dinner felt like a reunion of friends who had known each other for years rather than days. Return guests often said it was the Timberton Hotel that made it feel that way. But Mist knew it wasn't the hotel itself. Rather it was the people, the energy that they created themselves as they interacted. The brief respite from everyday life allowed them time to reflect, time to discover new interests or to rekindle those of earlier days.

As the dinner itself wound down, guests moved into the front parlor, where a roaring fire waited along with coffee, brandy, and other assorted after-dinner drinks appropriate for various ages. Whitney was pleased to see hot chocolate, and the professor eyed his favorite English tea with approval.

A piano stood waiting, sheet music spread above the keyboard, but this year's guests seemed more inclined toward further conversation than joining in song. Seeing this, Mist looked around for Michael, hoping he could attend to the sound system while she invited guests to help themselves to drinks of their choice. Not seeing any sign of him, she put on a playlist of Christmas favorites by Bing Crosby, Nat King Cole, and others, and then circled the room, making sure everyone was content with food, drink, music, and company.

Clive, per his yearly tradition, beckoned Betty over to the Christmas tree, where he lifted a new handcrafted ornament out of a hidden spot within the branches.

"It's beautiful!" Betty exclaimed as she held the silver stocking in the air. Tiny Yogo sapphires—these red, as sapphires came in all colors—twinkled as berries from within a holly branch design that ran across the top of the stocking.

"A wonderful Christmas Eve, as always," Clara said as Mist passed by.

"Here, here!" Andrew, standing beside Clara, raised his drink in the air.

"Oh, and..." Clara stood and leaned toward Mist, whispering. "You're going to find this amusing. Daniel's favorite toy as a child was Mr. Potato Head. You should have seen the professor's face when he said it!"

"Ah, and what about the professor?"

"A toy bus, one of those red double-decker ones they have in London."

Smiling, Mist continued to make the rounds, finally joining Betty in the archway that separated the front parlor from the lobby, where they could observe the gathering. Hotel guests and townsfolk alike, content and cheerful after the splendid dinner, relaxed near the fireplace, by the Christmas tree, and in cozy groups throughout the room. With music filling the room, and warm beverages filling the mugs many held, a sense of peace and warmth had settled over the crowd. It was exactly as Mist and Betty hoped every time they prepared for the holiday season.

"It's such a lovely evening, Mist," Betty said. "Especially with the storm over. Guests are looking forward to getting outside for Christmas Day."

Mist nodded. "There's a unique sense of holiday magic in the air."

"Exactly," Betty said. She cleared her throat. "You should see the votives we put outside."

"Really?" Mist glanced at Betty, surprised. It was a wonderful idea, though it hadn't been planned. Then again, with the storm unrelenting, nothing outside had been planned.

"Oh yes!" Betty said with an extra touch of enthusiasm. "Clive and I thought it would be nice for guests to go outside later to see the stars. It's such a treat that the weather cleared up."

"That's a wonderful idea," Mist agreed. "We should tell the guests." She took a step into the front parlor only to feel Betty's hand on her arm.

"Not yet," Betty said quickly. "You should check them out first. It's not even that cold, though I'd grab that cape of yours on the way out. It's in the lobby."

Mist turned to Betty, eyeing the hotelkeeper with curiosity. "All right. I think I will." She headed to the coatrack regularly used by guests and found her burgundy cape, thinking it odd, as she was certain she hadn't placed it there earlier. Even stranger was the ivory rose pinned to the collar, satin ribbons trailing from the stem. She looked back at Betty as she drew the cape around her shoulders.

"Just go," Betty whispered.

THIRTEEN

Intrigued, Mist opened the front door and stepped out onto the porch, finding a trail of small votive lights leading down the steps to the snow-covered front yard. The path to the gazebo had been recently shoveled, and the flickering lights led in that direction. As she stepped forward to follow the lights, she noticed rose petals scattered along the way. Red rose petals, she noted, suddenly suspicious of the large inventory she'd seen at Maisie's.

The gazebo came into sight once she turned toward the side yard. Lanterns hung inside the structure's white latticework, illuminating the interior with the soft glow of candlelight. A dusting of snow covered the floor and benches.

A light breeze kicked up as Mist continued to approach, causing rose petals to swirl up in the air. Mist mused that it might be the beating of her heart sending the petals into flight. For in the middle of the fairy-tale scene, Michael stood waiting.

"This is amazing," Mist whispered as she climbed the steps to the gazebo.

"*You* are amazing." Michael reached for her hands, which she gladly offered as she came to stand in front of him.

"As are you," Mist said.

Michael raised one hand and brushed her cheek softly with his fingers. "From the first time I saw you, I knew my life had changed."

Mist smiled but found herself at a loss for words. He'd just described her feelings exactly. She could remember the exact moment she noticed him sitting in the armchair by the fireplace, book in hand. His casual posture, his gray-green eyes, his love of literature, all spoke to her heart.

"Those first couple of years after you came to the Timberton Hotel, I looked forward to Christmas all year because I knew I'd be able to see you," Michael continued. "Then the university position opened up in Missoula, which brought me closer, and I was able to see you more often, not just during the holidays."

"That has been wonderful," Mist said. "I've been ever grateful that position opened up. I, too, was yearning for each Christmas to arrive so that I could see you."

"And now…" Michael's voice trailed off as he lowered himself to one knee. He reached for a jacket pocket, patted it, determined it was empty, and then reached for the other one, finding nothing there either. A third attempt proved successful as he pulled a small box from an inside pocket. Mist recognized it as one from Clive's gallery.

Michael shuffled his stance awkwardly, limited by his humble position.

Mist tilted her head to the side and looked down at the ground. "How does your knee feel?"

"Cold," Michael admitted, laughing.

"Perhaps you should stand up," Mist suggested with a smile.

"Perhaps I should," Michael stood back up and grinned. He brushed a light covering of snow off his knee, fumbling nervously, which Mist found not only amusing but charming.

"So, I was thinking, well, hoping..."

"Yes," Mist said softly.

"Yes?" Michael repeated. "I haven't even asked you anything."

"It doesn't matter."

"Why is that?"

"Because the answer is yes, whatever you're going to ask."

"That's a little risky, don't you think?" Michael smiled.

"Life is full of risks," Mist said.

"Well, I suppose that's true." Michael looked at the box in his hand, as if surprised to find it there. Regrouping, he opened it up and took out a ring that bore all the markings of Clive's expert handiwork. The exquisite design caused Mist to gasp, an exceedingly rare occurrence. Sculpted leaves in white gold surrounded a brilliant Yogo sapphire. Petite diamonds peeked out between several of the leaves, adding a touch of additional sparkle.

"It's beautiful." Mist tried to catch her breath as Michael slipped the ring on her finger. "A perfect design." She held her hand out, palm down, and let the light of the gazebo's lanterns reflect against the stones.

"I wanted something representative of the outdoors since you're so in tune with nature," Michael said. "That led to the idea of leaves. Clive suggested a Yoga sapphire since it's representative of the local area. And the tiny diamonds represent… I'm not sure what."

Mist took Michael's hand and led him down the steps of the gazebo. She held her hand out again and looked up. "This is what they represent." Michael followed her gaze, and together they took in the night. Where only storm clouds had been before, now bright stars dotted the sky.

"It's remarkable, all this starlight," Michael said, turning to Mist. "Just like you."

"We are all remarkable in our own way," Mist said.

"And you and I are remarkable together." Michael placed his hands on Mist's shoulders. He drew her closer and softly kissed her lips, lingering a few passionate seconds before stepping back. "So, does this mean you'll marry me?"

Mist laughed. "Of course. I already said yes."

FOURTEEN

Mist settled in front of the easel in her room, the one she'd lived in since losing the Moonglow Café's original building to a fire six years before. Betty's offer to move the café business into the hotel, as well as to give Mist the small room in the back hallway, had been a lifesaver at the time, and not just for her. Running the hotel on her own had become difficult for Betty. The chance to combine businesses and work tasks had come at a perfect time for both.

Now, staring at the small canvases in front of her, Mist contemplated not only final decisions about the miniature paintings she was creating but also the life she'd lived for the past six years as well as the one that lay ahead. And what would that be? Michael's proposal had been unexpected yet, in her heart, felt perfectly right. A discussion about this new life together would certainly come soon. Not on a holiday night with the hotel filled with guests, as they had known the night before, but soon.

Alone with those thoughts, Mist sorted through the paint colors she'd use to finish the guests' gifts. She treasured the tradition she'd started years ago of giving each guest a miniature painting to take home with them, a reminder of a special Christmas in Timberton.

Each color seemed to take on a double meaning as she chose which to use for which images. Brown might remind her of a guest's favorite childhood toy yet also represent a future home with Michael. Blue might represent the sky in a guest painting yet inspire thoughts of a quilt to make for times when she and Michael might sit together reading on a sofa, the quilt spread over their laps to provide warmth. Each color she chose to use for the guests hinted of something in her future, as if she could simply paint the time to come any way she liked.

Even as much of a dreamer as she was, Mist knew there were practical considerations to everything. Had Michael thought about where they would live? She knew he would never ask her to leave the Timberton Hotel or the Moonglow Café, so perhaps the faculty housing for the new outreach program would be his suggestion. Maybe this was why he hadn't said much about where the housing would be. For the sake of running the hotel and café efficiently, she hoped it would be in Timberton itself or else very close by.

Looking back, Mist could see clues she'd missed that something was in the works. Michael's nervousness, which she took as preoccupation with the new university program, now made more sense. Betty's happy encouragement about dressing up for Christmas Eve played right along with her excitement over the weather clearing before that night. And Maisie's overstock of red roses! She knew Maisie never ordered that many of one particular flower, not without a specific reason. If only she'd known what that reason would turn out to be.

Paintbrush in hand, Mist laughed out loud. She'd overlooked so many signs that now made sense. How long had this romantic proposal been planned? And how many people were in on it? Plenty, she knew, based on the cheers and applause she and Michael had received when they walked back into the hotel.

A soft knock on the door startled her. Not only was it now past midnight, but anyone who knew her was aware this was one night she worked alone, putting finishing touches on the paintings.

She set her paintbrush aside, stepped softly across the floor, and opened the door. To her surprise, Whitney stood in the hallway in flannel pajamas and bare feet, crutches under one arm, a sheet of paper in her free hand. Mist fought back a smile, not wanting to seem too approving of the girl being out in the hotel, barefoot, after midnight. But she was far more intrigued than worried. When a piece of paper—as she suspected—sends someone out into a hotel in the middle of the night, it must be important.

Mist leaned forward and whispered, "And what do we have here?" She lowered her gaze to the paper, which was facing away from her, and then back to Whitney's face.

"I wanted to show you this." Whitney handed the paper to Mist, who turned it toward her and smiled. The sketch of a tree was almost identical to the painting they'd both discussed in the front parlor, except the branches were more developed than the one Mist had portrayed.

"This is wonderful, Whitney."

"I made the branches stronger on top. Well, not on top, but on the sides. Well, not really on the sides, but mostly in the middle."

"I see," Mist said, admiring the branches' lines. "I like it. It's a strong tree."

"You can climb higher in this one." Whitney pointed to the middle and upper branches.

Mist looked at the girl, amazed yet somehow not at all surprised. The sweet child had a gift, not only for art but for life.

"You're right," Mist said. "I imagine you can climb as high as you want in this tree. Even in trees you haven't drawn yet." She handed the sketch back.

"I think so," Whitney agreed, taking the paper. "I'm going to draw a whole forest when I get back home."

"I believe you will," Mist said. "But I'm curious about something… How did you manage to get out of your room without your mother knowing?"

Whitney eyed her with caution, and Mist realized she probably thought she'd broken a rule.

"You're not in trouble," Mist assured her. "I'm just curious."

"You gave us two rooms," Whitney said.

"Ah, so I did. The suite with two rooms and a sitting area in between. I can see it would be possible to escape from there."

"An art escape!" Whitney said, clearly excited by the concept.

Mist smiled. "Yes, an art escape. And now I suspect sneaking back into your room would be wise."

Whitney nodded. "I know. I just wanted to show you."

"I'm glad you did," Mist said. "And I promise to keep this midnight expedition our little secret."

"Thanks," Whitney whispered. "Bye." She hobbled off down the hallway, taking care to place her crutches soundlessly on the wooden floor.

Mist closed the door and returned to her own project. Not only had Whitney's visit been delightful—in a sneaky, forbidden way—it had been inspiring. Picking up her paintbrush again, Mist set to work with joy and abandon.

FIFTEEN

Christmas morning arrived with a clear message: the storm was gone for good, or at least until the next one arrived. Where stars had filled the sky the night before, rays of sunshine flowed down upon Timberton, bathing the town in light and warmth. It was a postcard-perfect winter scene, exactly what guests needed after being inside for days.

Mist rose even earlier than usual, unable to sleep in spite of painting until the early hours of the morning. By five thirty a.m., coffee perked, tea steeped, and lemon-poppyseed muffins baked in the oven. Mist had just begun sweeping the café when Clive stopped in for his usual first caffeine infusion. She noted that, for the first time in weeks, he was not dressed for construction. At least he would be taking Christmas Day to relax.

"Let me see that hand, my dear," Clive said as soon as his mug was filled with steaming coffee.

Setting the broom aside, Mist held out what she knew he wanted to see: the sapphire ring that he'd so beautifully crafted. Under the café lights, the deep blue gemstone and tiny "stars" sparkled with the promise of a joyful Christmas morning and blessed years to come.

"It's exquisite, Clive," Mist said. "I'm honored to wear what is truly a piece of art from an artist I adore."

"You're not going to get all mushy on me now, are you?" Clive protested. "It's just a bit of metal and rock, you know."

"It's so much more than that," Mist said, admiring the one-of-a-kind ring again, just as she'd done many times since the night before. "It is joy and hope and wishes and dreams."

"And metal and rock," Clive said. He took a gulp of coffee and turned as Betty stepped into the café. "Another early bird, I see." He offered her a cup of coffee and then refilled his own.

"I couldn't sleep," Betty said. "There's just so much excitement in the air!" She exchanged a kiss with Clive and then gave Mist a hug. "Did you sleep at all, Mist?"

"Not much," Mist admitted, laughing. "Maybe an hour or two. I'll catch up when things settle down."

"I doubt that'll be today," Betty said. "Guests will be up and around soon, and I know some of the townsfolk will be stopping by to congratulate you and Michael."

"Am I the only one who didn't know this was planned?" Mist asked.

"Maybe," Betty said with mock seriousness before laughing. "No, only a few people knew. Well, maybe a dozen or so."

"You'd be surprised what secrets people can keep around here," Clive said. Mist noted that he and Betty exchanged glances. "By the way, what's for breakfast?"

"A simple assortment of granola, fresh fruit, yogurt, juice, and lemon-poppyseed muffins, which are due out of the oven right about now." Mist headed for the kitchen, Clive and Betty right behind her.

"I could fry up some bacon and eggs if anyone wants real food," Clive offered as he took a seat at the center island.

Mist laughed. "That sounds like an excellent idea, Clive. We'll give guests the option, and you can be the short-order chef."

"It's a deal." Clive grinned.

"I'm not sure how hungry people will be after last night's feast," Betty said. "I'll be lucky if I can manage granola and fruit." She watched Mist pull the muffins out of the oven. "Although... I think I could find room for one of those. They smell delicious!"

"They certainly do," Clive said. "Maybe we need to try them. All in the name of quality control, of course."

"How about splitting one and leaving the rest for the guests?" Betty suggested.

Clive shrugged. "I suppose that's fair."

Mist pulled one of the muffins from the pan for them and placed the others in a woven basket, which she took into the café along with the other dishes for the breakfast buffet. She propped the café door open so guests could wander in at their leisure and then made a quick trip to her room, returning with small packages wrapped in rice paper and raffia, which she slipped between the branches of the Christmas tree in the front parlor.

Clive, having given his approval to the muffins, busied himself getting a fire going while Betty chose classic carols for the sound system. By the time guests began to emerge, the hotel stood ready with a plentiful buffet, holiday music, dancing flames in the fireplace, and coffee, tea, and hot chocolate, marshmallows and whipped cream included. To top it off, the Christmas tree sparkled with twinkling lights and beckoned with gifts those staying at the hotel had placed underneath the night before.

One or two at a time, the guests gathered in the café, offering Christmas greetings to each other and enjoying the buffet offerings. Clive proudly made bacon and eggs for those who took him up on the "real food" option. Whitney had two hot chocolates, the professor had his usual tea, and all had muffins along with other items of their choice.

Moving the celebration to the front parlor, guests settled in, many exchanging gifts. Clara and Andrew had brought presents for each other; Stephen and Erika had done the same, as had Nora and Whitney. After a flurry of wrapping paper, tissue, and ribbons, each guest had at least one new possession.

As rounds of *thank you* and *you shouldn't have* and *how did you know* circled the room, Mist pulled the small rice paper and raffia-wrapped packages from within the tree's branches, passed them out, and encouraged the guests to open them.

"It's my train!" Andrew exclaimed as he pulled the miniature painting from the rice paper. "And it looks just like I remember it!"

"So does my bear!" Nora held her painting up for everyone to see. Clara did the same, showing off her microscope, and the professor followed with his red double-decker bus. Stephen's eyes grew wide at the painting of a blue model airplane with a lightning bolt on its side, and Erika wiped a tear away as she smiled at the tiny horse reflected on a painted mirror.

Daniel drew the biggest response when he unveiled his Mr. Potato Head, and to Mist's delight, he laughed heartily along with the group.

Whitney was the last to show her painting, though she had been the first to tear off the wrapping. While the others had shared theirs, she'd kept hers hugged to her chest, a big smile on her face. When she finally turned it around for everyone to see, various puzzled expressions looked back at her.

Erika leaned forward to get a closer look. "What kind of favorite toy is that?"

"It's not a toy, it's a tree," Whitney said, beaming.

"A very tall tree," Mist said.

"With strong branches," Whitney added.

Nora looked closely at the painting her daughter held. "There's a girl sitting on top of the tree… holding a paintbrush?"

"I think that's me." Whitney turned to Mist. "Right?"

Mist nodded. "I believe it is. The branches look strong enough for you to reach the top."

"It's perfect," Whitney said.

Michael, who had been sitting next to Mist, whispered, "wonderful" into her ear, and left the room. Within minutes, the miniature paintings were set aside to be treasured later, and the guests began to mingle.

Pleased to see the group refilling drinks and falling back into conversation, Mist headed for the kitchen with the intention of helping with dishes so Betty wouldn't be stuck doing them all. Just as she reached the kitchen door, Clive called to her from the lobby.

"Mist? I could use your help with something."

Mist turned toward Clive. "My help? Of course. Whatever you need."

"You'll need a coat," Clive said.

"Or your cape," Betty added, having emerged from the kitchen at the sound of Clive's voice. "It's still on the coatrack in the lobby."

"Coat or cape? I take it we're going outside. To the gallery, maybe?"

"Maybe," Clive said with a grin Mist perceived as mischievous.

"Why don't I come help too." Betty ducked into the kitchen to grab the jacket she kept on a hook near the side entrance, returning quickly with it on.

As the three headed for the front door, Mist glanced in the living room to see if Michael had shown up again. Not seeing him, she followed Clive and Betty outside.

SIXTEEN

Mist followed Clive outside, expecting him to turn left at the sidewalk in the direction of the gallery. Instead, he turned right, toward the old café location. Mist, walking side by side with Betty, gave her an inquisitive look. In return, Betty simply smiled.

It only took a minute to arrive at the rustic building where Mist had first started feeding the townsfolk. Mist stood still, remembering when she first arrived in Timberton, the many meals prepared and served there, the small room in the back where she'd lived and painted, and the night when, standing in the same spot she was now, she'd watched it burn. As hard as Clayton and his crew had tried to save it, the damage had been too extensive to save the café.

"Thank you," Mist said, turning to Betty. "For giving me a room in the hotel and a new home for the Moonglow Café."

Betty shook her head. "You have no idea what you gave in return, do you? I simply gave you two rooms. You brought the hotel to life, the whole *town* to life, really. You feed us, you inspire us with your art, you bring us together. You turned a small Montana town into a community."

"She's right, Mist," Clive said, having walked ahead to the front door. "I'm not one for fancy speeches, so I'll just say Betty is right, everything she just said."

"You're both very kind," Mist said, taking in the reconstructed exterior, freshly painted walls, gleaming window panes, and new front door with beveled glass window. "And the building looks wonderful!"

"I'm so glad you think so," Clive said. "That's why I need your help."

"Of course," Mist said, just as she'd said at first. "What can I do?"

Clive reached into his pocket and pulled out a key. "You can help me open it."

He dangled the key from his fingers, and Mist walked forward and took it. A rush of emotion flowed through her at the thought of entering her old building, so filled with memories. Her only regret at the moment was that Michael was not there to share it.

Mist inserted the key in the door and turned it without a problem, making her realize—as she already suspected—that Clive didn't really need help. This was just his clever way of showing her the building, as he had promised during construction. But when she opened the door, she was stunned by what she saw. Instead of an empty, remodeled room, a cozy living room greeted her, complete with polished hardwood floors, a plush couch, and a large throw rug under a coffee table. And the biggest surprise of all was the sight of Michael sitting in a wingback chair in front of a fireplace.

Michael looked up and grinned as Mist opened her mouth, found herself at a loss for words, and closed it again. "Welcome to faculty housing," he said.

"Faculty housing?" Mist glanced at Clive and Betty, who both fought back grins as they shrugged their shoulders.

"Okay," Michael said. He stood and approached her, placing his hands gently on her shoulders. "It's not officially faculty housing. Actually, there isn't any faculty housing."

Mist looked around at Betty, Clive, and Michael. "You all seem to be very good at keeping secrets."

"I was a little worried when you asked to see it," Clive admitted.

Mist laughed. "Your explanation of construction liability and safety factors was convincing."

"I was counting on that," Clive said.

"Come see the rest." Michael took her elbow gently and led her into other rooms, which were beautifully finished yet empty. "I thought you'd want to choose furnishings. Even the living room can be changed if you want something different. We just wanted it to feel like home when you walked in."

"The living room is lovely just the way it is," Mist said.

"And I didn't dare touch the kitchen."

"That will be a joy to set up." She kissed Michael and then led the way to the living room, where Betty and Clive were waiting.

"You'll still have your room at the hotel, of course," Betty said. "You can use it as an art studio or to rest while working or even to escape from this crazy literature teacher with all these tricks up his sleeve." She smiled as she glanced at Michael.

"That's wonderful," Mist said. She brought her hands to her face as she looked around. "I'm overwhelmed. You've all gone to so much work and planning. I thank you from every corner of my heart. Perhaps we should get back to the guests for now. What do you think?" She turned to Michael. "We can come back over here later."

"Sounds like a good plan," Michael said.

Together, all four walked back to the hotel, where they found the guests enjoying activities and conversation.

Nora sat at the crafts table with Whitney, rubbing her daughter's back. "You didn't disappoint me at all! I only want you to be happy. If dance isn't it, and art is, that's fine! In fact, that's wonderful. The sketches and painting you've done here are amazing."

"It makes me happy, Mom."

"That's all that matters." Nora pulled Whitney into an embrace.

Mist joined Clara by the Christmas tree where she was admiring the ornament Clive had given Betty the night before.

"There you are, dear!" Clara exclaimed. "How did you like the old café building?"

Mist laughed. "Truly, am I the only one who didn't know about all these surprises?"

"I doubt it," Clara said. "I'm pretty sure Wild Bill didn't know. He's been occupied trying to learn how to make that frittata of yours. I think he's on his eighth attempt at this point. Maybe the tenth. And then there's... Well, I'm not sure who else, but there must be more who didn't know."

Mist spotted Daniel across the room, engaged in a lively discussion with the professor. "Dr. Hutton is finally relaxed," she said. "This wasn't an easy Christmas for him, worrying about those test results."

"No, it wasn't."

"It must be hard to be both doctor and patient." Mist looked at Clara.

"Ah, you figured it out," Clara said. "Yes, the doctor was the patient this time."

"I'm so glad he received good news. Just another little Christmas miracle."

"You seem to get a lot of those here," Clara pointed out. "Erika rekindled her joy of teaching, thanks to Hollister."

Mist smiled, seeing Erika and Stephen in a conversation with Hollister, who held a cup of hot cocoa in his hands. "I doubt she really wanted to retire early. Sometimes we just need something to remind us where we're meant to be."

"Well, I can tell you where we're all meant to be at Christmas," Clara said. "Here at the Timberton Hotel."

"Yes," Mist replied. "I do believe that's true."

"I wonder who we'll have here a year from now," Betty pondered as she joined them.

Mist smiled. "We'll just have to see next Christmas."

———

Betty's Cookie Exchange Recipes

Glazed Cinnamon Nuts
Santa's Favorite Chocolate Cookies
Eggnog Cookies with Rum Butter Icing
Apple Pie Cookies
Cherry Scones
Aunt Nellie's Peanut Butter Surprise
Christmas Snow Clouds
Whipped Chocolate Chip Shortbread Cookies
Sugar-free Orange Cookies
Cranberry White Chocolate Bars
Rhubarb Cookies
Cherry Brownie Bonbons
Impossible Peanut Butter Cookies
Caramel Popcorn Balls
Mom's Angel Pie
Amish Sugar Cookies
Grinch Cookies
Chai Tea Shortbread Cookies
Nutella Hazelnut Brownies
Peanut Butter Chocolate Fudge
Christmas Dreams

GLAZED CINNAMON NUTS
(a family recipe)

Ingredients:

1 cup sugar
1/4 cup water
1/8 teaspoon cream of tartar
Heaping teaspoon of cinnamon
1 tablespoon butter
1-1/2 cups walnut halves

Directions:

Boil sugar, water, cream of tartar, and cinnamon to soft boil stage (236 degrees).

Remove from heat.

Add butter and walnuts.

Stir until walnuts separate.

Place on waxed paper to cool.

SANTA'S FAVORITE CHOCOLATE COOKIES

(Submitted by Kim Davis of *Cinnamon and Sugar and a Little Bit of Murder* blog)

Ingredients:

1-1/4 cups unsalted butter, room temperature
2 cups granulated sugar
2 eggs, room temperature
1 tablespoon pure vanilla extract
1/2 teaspoon espresso powder (or instant coffee such as Starbucks)
3/4 cup Dutch cocoa powder
2 cups all-purpose flour
1 teaspoon baking soda
1 teaspoon salt
*Coarse white sugar or peppermint crunch baking chips for garnish

Directions:

In a medium bowl, sift together the cocoa powder, all-purpose flour, baking soda, and salt. Set aside.

In the bowl of a standing mixer, beat the butter and sugar together until creamy, about 3 minutes.

Beat in the eggs, one at time, until fully incorporated. Mix in the vanilla.

Slowly add the dry ingredients to the butter and sugar mixture. Mix just until fully incorporated.

Separate the dough into two pieces and roll each piece into 12-inch logs (about 2 inches in diameter). Tightly wrap each log in parchment paper.

Refrigerate for at least 2 hours or overnight.

Preheat the oven to 350 degrees.

Slice the cookies into 1/2-inch-thick rounds and place on a parchment-lined baking sheet. Sprinkle tops of cookies with coarse white sugar or peppermint crunch baking chips.

Bake for 10 minutes, rotating pan once halfway through baking cycle.

Allow to cool on the baking sheet for 5 minutes, then remove to a wire rack to cool completely.

Store in an airtight container at room temperature for up to three days.

Tips: If dough is too hard to slice through, allow to sit at room temperature for 15–30 minutes.

The dough can be made up to 3 months ahead of time, formed into logs, and wrapped in parchment paper. Place the logs into a freezer-safe plastic bag and freeze until needed. Allow the frozen dough to defrost overnight in the refrigerator, then proceed as directed for slicing and baking.

EGGNOG COOKIE WITH RUM BUTTER ICING
(Submitted by Jeannie Daniel)

Ingredients:

1 stick unsalted butter, softened
1 cup dark brown sugar, packed
1 large egg
2/3 cup eggnog
2 cups flour
1/2 teaspoon baking soda
1/2 teaspoon salt
1/2 teaspoon nutmeg
1/2 teaspoon ginger
Nutmeg for garnish, optional

Directions:

Preheat over to 350 degrees.

Cream butter, brown sugar, until creamy. Add in egg, mix, then add eggnog.

In a separate bowl, combine all the dry ingredients. Sift or whisk to mix well.

Add dry ingredients to eggnog mixture. Mix well.

Scoop a level 1/4 cup measure and place on greased cookie sheet 2 inches apart.

Bake for 15 minutes.

When the cookies are cooled, mix 1/4 cup butter, 1-1/2 cups powdered sugar, and 3 tablespoons rum or 2 tablespoons rum extract.

Melt the butter in a saucepan, then transfer to a bowl with the rum.

Stir in powdered sugar, 1/2 cup at a time, blending each addition until smooth.

Set it aside to thicken a little bit and spread into cooled cookies.

Dust with nutmeg or cinnamon to decorate.

These keep well in a tight-fitting container. They can also be refrigerated.

APPLE PIE COOKIES

(Submitted by Carol Anderson)

Ingredients:

1/2 cup shortening or butter
1 cup coconut sugar
1 egg substitute
1 teaspoon vanilla extract
1/2 cup apple, chopped fine
1 cup all-purpose flour
1/4 cup wheat flour
1/2 teaspoon sea salt
2 teaspoons baking powder

Directions:

Cream sugar and shortening. Add egg substitute, vanilla, and apples.

Mix dry ingredients together and add to above.

Scoop by tablespoon, roll into balls, roll in sugar mix.

Bake at 350 degrees for 10–12 minutes.

CHERRY SCONES

(Submitted by Kris Bock from *The Southwest Armchair Traveler* blog)

Ingredients:

1/2 cup dried cherries, cranberries, or currents
1/2 apple juice or grape juice
2 cups flour
1/4 cup sugar
1/2 teaspoon baking soda
2 teaspoons baking powder
1/2 teaspoon salt
1/2 teaspoon nutmeg
1/4 cup cold butter
1 egg
1/2 cup plain yogurt (full-fat preferred)
1 teaspoon lemon or orange zest

Directions:

Preheat oven to 375°.

Soak cherries in juice for at least 10 minutes while you mix other ingredients.

Mix the flour and 1/4 cup of the sugar. Blend in the baking soda, baking powder, salt, and nutmeg.

Cut in the butter with a pastry blender or two knives until the mixture has fine crumbs.

Stir in the egg, yogurt, and zest. Drain the cherries or other dried fruit well. Mix them in.

Spray a baking sheet lightly with oil.

Turn the dough onto the baking sheet. Pat it down into a 9-inch circle.

Cut the dough into 8 wedges. Separate them slightly. You may sprinkle with additional sugar if you want them to sparkle a bit.

Bake until golden and firm, about 20 minutes.

Serve warm with butter, clotted cream, orange marmalade, or jam.

*This recipe also works well with dried cranberries or currents.

Aunt Nellie's PB Surprise
(Submitted by Petrenia Etheridge)

Ingredients:

Ritz crackers
Peanut butter
Marshmallows

Directions:

Spread peanut butter on Ritz crackers, salt side down, and place on cookie sheet about 2 inches apart. Add a marshmallow to the top of each.

Bake at 350 until marshmallows swell and are lightly brown.

Remove from oven and let them deflate. Serve with hot cocoa while still warm.

CHRISTMAS SNOW CLOUDS
(Submitted by Petrenia Etheridge)
(Cream cheese teacake puffs)

Ingredients:

1 egg
1/2 cup salted butter
4 oz. cream cheese
1/2-1 cup sugar, depends on desired sweetness
1-1/4 cups cake flour
1/2 teaspoon baking powder
1 teaspoon vanilla extract
1 teaspoon rum, almond or lemon extract

Directions:

Make sure first 3 ingredients are room temperature. Cream together butter and cream cheese until well blended, then add sugar and blend well.

Add in egg and extracts until well incorporated. Fork cake flour and baking powder separately, then add slowly and blend gently. Chill mixture 1–2 hours.

Preheat oven to 375 and line baking sheet with parchment paper. Spoon 1–2-inch balls into paper with a floured spoon. Slightly press with a floured cup but not flat or they won't puff up.

Bake for 8-10 minutes until bottoms are slightly brown. Decorate with your favorite icing when cool or just top with confectioners' sugar or sprinkles.

WHIPPED CHOCOLATE CHIP SHORTBREAD COOKIES
(Submitted by Shelia Hall)

Ingredients:

1 cup butter, room temperature
1-1/2 cups all-purpose flour
1/2 cup powdered sugar
1 cup chocolate chips

Directions:

In a mixing bowl, (or bowl from stand mixer) on low-speed blend butter, all-purpose flour, and icing sugar for 1 minute.

Increase speed to medium and mix for seven minutes.

Add in chocolate chips by hand, mixing only until combined, being gentle when mixing.

Using a cookie scoop or heaping tablespoon, drop onto baking sheets 12 to a sheet.

Bake in 350F oven for 10-12 minutes until edges are just light golden brown, being careful not to overbake.

Remove from oven and cool at least five minutes before transferring to a wire cooling rack.

Store cookies in an airtight container for up to five days or in refrigerator container for up to ten days.

SUGAR-FREE ORANGE COOKIES
(Submitted by Brenda Ellis)

Ingredients:

1-1/2 cups all-purpose flour
1 teaspoon baking powder
Sugar substitute equal to 3/4 cup sugar
2 teaspoons grated orange zest
1/4 teaspoon salt
1/8 teaspoon ground nutmeg
1/2 cup vegetable oil spread
1/3 cup chopped golden raisins
1/4 cup egg substitute
2 tablespoons orange juice

Directions:

Combine first 6 ingredients. Cut in spread until mixture resembles coarse crumbs.

Stir in raisins.

Add egg substitute and orange juice.

Mix well.

Drop by teaspoonfuls onto baking sheet coated with cooking spray.

Flatten with a fork coated with flour.

Bake at 375 for 13–15 minutes.

Remove and let cool on cooling rack.

CRANBERRY WHITE CHOCOLATE BARS
(Submitted by Molly Elliott)

Ingredients:

2 large eggs
1/2 teaspoon vanilla extract
1 cup sugar
1 cup all-purpose flour
1/4 teaspoon salt
1/2 cup butter, melted
3/4 cups fresh or frozen (thawed) cranberries, coarsely chopped
1/2 (11-oz) bag white chocolate chips

Directions:

Preheat oven to 350 degrees.

Whisk together eggs and vanilla extract in a mixing bowl until blended.

Gradually add sugar, beating until blended.

Stir in flour, salt, and melted butter.

Gently stir in cranberries and white chocolate chips.

Spread dough in a lightly greased 8-inch square pan.

Bake 38 to 40 minutes or until a toothpick inserted in center comes out clean.

Cool and cut into bars.

RHUBARB COOKIES

(Submitted by Brenda Brodmerkel)

Ingredients:

1 cup butter, softened
2 eggs
1 cup sugar
1/2 cup brown sugar
2 teaspoons vanilla extract
2-1/2 cups flour
1 teaspoon baking powder
1/2 teaspoon salt

Directions:

Preheat oven to 400 degrees.

In mixing bowl, cream together with 2 eggs, 1 cup soft butter, 1 cup sugar, 1/2 cup brown sugar, and 2 teaspoons vanilla.

Mix in separate bowl 2-1/2 cups flour, 1 tsp. baking powder, 1/2 tsp. salt.

Add to wet mixture.

Add 1 cup white choc chips and 2 cups cut-up rhubarb.

Drop by spoonful onto baking sheet and bake for 14 minutes.

CHERRY BROWNIE BON BONS
(Submitted by Vera Kenyon)

Ingredients:

1 fudge brownie mix
1/4 cup Kirschwasser / cherry brandy or 1/4 cup water
1/4 cup vegetable oil
1 egg
2 10 oz. jars maraschino cherries with stems
1/2 cup powdered sugar
Chocolate Fudge Filling
1 3 oz. pkg cream cheese
1 teaspoon vanilla
1/4 cup light corn syrup
3 squares of unsweetened chocolate, melted and cooled
1 cup powdered sugar

Directions:

Preheat oven to 350.

Stir brownie mix, Kirschwasser, oil, and egg in a bowl 50 strokes until well blended.

Fill greased, miniature muffin cups two-thirds full of brownie batter.

Bake for 15 minutes or until a wooden toothpick comes out with fudgy crumbs. Be careful not to overbake.

Cool slightly and remove from the muffin pans. While the brownies are still warm, put them on a waxed-paper-lined tray.

Make a half-inch indentation into each brownie with the end of a wooden spoon. Cool completely.

Prepare the chocolate fudge filling. For the filling, beat cream cheese and vanilla in a small bowl. Slowly pour in the corn syrup, then add chocolate and beat until smooth. Gradually add the powdered sugar and blend well.

When the filling is prepared, drain the cherries, reserving the liquid. Let the cherries sit on a paper towel to dry.

Combine the powdered sugar with enough reserved liquid to form a thin glaze.

Spoon or pipe about one teaspoon of the chocolate fudge into the indentation of each brownie.

Gently press a cherry into the filling. Drizzle with the sugar glaze.

IMPOSSIBLE PEANUT BUTTER COOKIES
(Submitted by Mary Elizabeth Terberg)

Ingredients:

1 cup creamy peanut butter
1 cup sugar
1 egg
1 teaspoon vanilla

Directions:

Mix all ingredients together.

Drop by spoonful on ungreased cookie sheet.

Press each cookie with a fork greased with butter and dipped in sugar.

Bake at 325 degrees for 10–12 minutes.

Let cool on cookie sheet.

Makes 18.

CARAMEL POPCORN BALLS
(Submitted by Betty Escobar)

Ingredients:

1 cup butter
1 cup brown sugar
1/2 cup light corn syrup
2/3 cup (1/2 15 oz. can) sweetened condensed milk
1/2 teaspoon vanilla
5 quarts popcorn

Directions:

In saucepan, combine all ingredients except condensed milk and vanilla.

Bring to boil over medium heat, stirring well.

Stir in condensed milk and simmer, stirring constantly, until it reaches soft ball stage (234–238).

Stir in vanilla.

Pour over popcorn and mix. Butter hands and form into balls approx. 3-1/2 inches.

Makes 15.

MOM'S ANGEL PIE
(Submitted by Pat Decoster)

Ingredients:

8 eggs, separated into whites and yolks
3 cups sugar separated into 2 cup and 1 cup portions
1 teaspoon cream of tartar
1/4 cup lemon juice

Directions:

Beat 8 egg whites until frothy.

Slowly add 2 cups of sugar and cream of tartar.

Spread into 9 x 13-inch pan and bake at 300 degrees for 20 minutes.

Turn oven down to 250 degrees and bake another 40 minutes.

Beat 8 egg yolks well with 1 cup sugar and lemon juice. Cook in double broiler until thick.

Allow to cool, then spread over bottom layer and cover with whipped cream or Cool Whip.

Amish Sugar Cookies
(Submitted by Alma Collins)

Ingredients:

4-1/2 cups all-purpose flour
1 teaspoon baking soda
1 teaspoon salt
1 cup sugar
1 cup powdered sugar
2 eggs
1 cup oil
1 cup butter
1 teaspoon vanilla

Directions:

Mix together flour, baking soda, and salt, and set aside.

Cream together sugar, powdered sugar, eggs, oil, butter, and vanilla. Add flour mixture.

Roll into balls and place on an ungreased cookie sheet.

Grease bottom of glass or cookie stamp and dip into sugar to press cookie.

Bake at 350° for 8–10 minutes. (Hint: Use seasonal cookie stamps and colored sugar.)

GRINCH COOKIES
(Submitted by Shelly Maynard)

Makes 24 cookies
Prep time: 10 minutes
Bake time: 9 minutes
Frosting time: 10 minutes

Ingredients:

1 box of white cake mix
2 large eggs
1/2 cup vegetable oil
1 cup powdered sugar
1 tablespoon milk
1 teaspoon vanilla
Green food coloring
Yellow food coloring
Red heart sprinkles

Directions:

Preheat the oven to 350 degrees.
Line a baking sheet with parchment paper.
Add cake mix, eggs, and vegetable oil to a large bowl and stir well.

Add equal amounts of green and yellow food coloring to get your desired "Grinch" color, about 4 drops of each.

Using a cookie scoop, drop scoops of dough onto a baking sheet, 1–2 inches apart.

Bake for 9 minutes. Remove from the oven and set the baking sheet on a wire cooling rack for one minute.

Remove cookies from the baking sheet onto the wire cooling rack. Allow cookies to cool completely.

Mix the powdered sugar, milk, and vanilla in a small bowl.

Add 2 drops each of green and yellow food coloring. Stir well.

Check the consistency. It should be just perfect—not too runny and not too thick.

Spread icing on the cookies.

Place a heart in the center of the cookies.

CHAI TEA SHORTBREAD COOKIES

(Submitted by Kris Bock from *The Southwest Armchair Traveler* blog)

**If using loose-leaf tea, grind the tea into a rough powder first. If using tea bags, cut open the tea bags (4–6) and measure. Tea bags usually have a more powdered mix, so you don't have to grind it. Mix the ingredients in a food processor for ease. You can also press the dough into a shortbread pan and bake for about 30 minutes.

Ingredients:

2 cups all-purpose flour
2/3 cup sugar
2 tablespoons chai tea (ground fine)
1/2 teaspoon salt
1 cup (2 sticks) butter, room temperature
2 teaspoons vanilla extract

Directions:

Preheat oven to 375 degrees.

Blend the flour, sugar, chai, and salt.

Mix in the butter and vanilla. Press the mixture into a ball of dough.

Roll out the dough on a floured surface to about 1/3-inch thick. Use a cookie cutter and place

cookies 2 inches apart on baking sheets lined with parchment paper or silicone baking sheets.

Bake until the edges are golden, 8–12 minutes depending on size.

Let cool on sheets for 5 minutes, then transfer to wire racks and cool to room temperature.

NUTELLA HAZELNUT BROWNIES
(Submitted by Katie Brown)

Ingredients:

1 and 1/2 cup Nutella or hazelnut spread
1/2 cup flour
2 eggs
1/2 tablespoon olive oil
2 to 4 oz halved hazelnuts
1/4 cup semi-sweet chocolate chips

Directions:

Preheat oven to 325 degrees.

Mix Nutella, flour, eggs, oil until well combined with beaters.

Stir in hazelnuts and chocolate chips. Spread into greased/olive oiled pan.

Bake 30 to 35 min until middle no longer jiggles when shaking the pan.

*For 8 x 8 glass pan, 38 minutes to get brownies still very moist and fudgy but cooked through.

Let cool slightly before serving or packaging individually.

PEANUT BUTTER CHOCOLATE FUDGE
(Submitted by Lena Winfrey Hayat)

Ingredients:

20 reg. size peanut butter cups
3 cups of chocolate chips
14 oz. can sweetened condensed milk

Directions:

Put 16 peanut butter cups facedown in a dish.

Mix milk and chocolate chips together. Microwave for 1 min. Stir and then microwave for another 3 to 5 min. until melted.

Pour mixture over peanut butter cups.

Break the last 4 peanut butter cups into pieces. Spread over top, gently pushing down into mixture.

Refrigerate until set. Cut into squares.

CHRISTMAS DREAMS
(Submitted by Colleen Galster)

Ingredients:

15 oz. box white cake mix
2 large eggs
1/3 cup cream soda
1/2 cup butterscotch chips
1/2 cup white chocolate chips
Optional: sprinkles

Directions:

Preheat oven to 350 and line cookie sheets with parchment paper.

Mix cake mix, eggs, and cream soda. Stir until fully combined.

Fold in butterscotch chips and white chocolate chips.

Scoop batter onto cookie sheets 2 inches apart. Add sprinkles if desired.

Bake for 8–10 minutes or until the middle sets and edges start to turn a light golden brown.

Let cool 10 minutes, then serve.

*Adapt with any flavor combination by choosing a different cake mix, clear soda, and mix-ins.

Acknowledgments

I'm grateful to the many people who help keep the spirit of Christmas alive each year in the Moonglow Christmas books. Starlight at Moonglow only exists because of top-notch editing by Annie Sarac, developmental help, beta reading, and support from Jay Garner, Karen Putnam, Elizabeth Christy, Sue Liebson, and Paul Sterrett. Lego Normarie and Tara Meyers deserve credit for formatting. The lovely cover design is by Keri Knutson with additional graphics work by Perry Kirkpatrick.

No Moonglow Christmas book would be complete without Betty's annual cookie exchange. The delicious recipes in this book are thanks to Kim Davis and her blog, *Cinnamon and Sugar and a Little Bit of Murder*, Jeannie Daniel, Petrenia Etheridge, Shelia Hall, Kris Bock and her blog, *The Southwest Armchair Traveler*, Brenda Ellis, Molly Elliott, Brenda Brodmerkle, Carol Anderson, Vera Kenyon, Mary Elizabeth Terberg, Betty Escobar, Pat Decoster, Alma Collins, Shelly Maynard, Katie Brown, Lena Winfrey Hayat, and Colleen Galster. Mist, Betty, and the rest of the gang hope you pick a recipe or two have some fun in the kitchen. Enjoy!

Recipe Notes

RECIPE NOTES

RECIPE NOTES

RECIPE NOTES

Books by Deborah Garner

The Paige MacKenzie Series

Above the Bridge

When NY reporter Paige MacKenzie arrives in Jackson Hole, it's not long before her instincts tell her there's more than a basic story to be found in the popular, northwestern Wyoming mountain area. A chance encounter with attractive cowboy Jake Norris soon has Paige chasing a legend of buried treasure passed down through generations. Side- stepping a few shady characters who are also searching for the same hidden reward, she will have to decide who is trustworthy and who is not.

The Moonglow Café

The discovery of an old diary inside the wall of the historic hotel soon sends NY reporter Paige MacKenzie into the underworld of art and deception. Each of the town's residents holds a key to untangling more than one long-buried secret, from the hippie chick owner of a new age café to the mute homeless man in the town park. As the worlds of western art and sapphire mining collide, Paige finds herself juggling research, romance, and danger.

Three Silver Doves

The New Mexico resort of Agua Encantada seems a perfect destination for reporter Paige MacKenzie to combine work with well-deserved rest and relaxation. But when suspicious jewelry shows up on another guest, and the town's storyteller goes missing, Paige's R&R is soon redefined as restlessness and risk. Will an unexpected overnight trip to Tierra Roja Casino lead her to the answers she seeks, or are darker secrets lurking along the way?

Hutchins Creek Cache

When a mysterious 1920's coin is discovered behind the Hutchins Creek Railroad Museum in Colorado, Paige MacKenzie starts digging into four generations of Hutchins family history, with a little help from the Denver Mint. As legends of steam engines and coin mintage mingle, will Paige discover the true origin of the coin, or will she find herself riding the rails dangerously close to more than one long- hidden town secret?

Crazy Fox Ranch

As Paige MacKenzie returns to Jackson Hole, she has only two things on her mind: enjoy life with Wyoming's breathtaking Grand Tetons as the backdrop and spend more time with handsome cowboy Jake Norris as he prepares to open his guest ranch. But when a stranger's odd behavior leads her to research western filming in the area—in particular, the movie Shane, will it simply lead to a freelance article for the Manhattan Post, or will it lead to a dangerous hidden secret?

Sweet Sierra Gulch

Paige MacKenzie isn't convinced there's anything "sweet" about Sweet Sierra Gulch when she arrives in the small California Gold Rush town. Still, there's plenty of history as well as anticipated romance with her favorite cowboy, Jake Norris. But when the owner of the local café goes missing, Paige is determined to find out why. Will she uncover a dangerous secret in the town's old mining tunnels, or will curiosity land her in over her head?

The Sadie Kramer Flair Series

A Flair for Chardonnay

When flamboyant senior sleuth Sadie Kramer learns the owner of her favorite chocolate shop is in trouble, she heads for the California wine country with a tote-bagged Yorkie and a slew of questions. The fourth generation Tremiato Winery promises answers, but not before a dead body turns up at the vintners' scheduled Harvest Festival. As Sadie juggles truffles, tips, and turmoil, she'll need to sort the grapes from the wrath in order to find the identity of the killer.

A Flair for Drama

When a former schoolmate invites Sadie Kramer to a theatre production, she jumps at the excuse to visit the Monterey Bay area for a weekend. Plenty of action is expected on stage, but when the show's leading lady turns up dead, Sadie finds herself faced with more than one drama to follow. With both cast members and production crew as potential suspects, will Sadie and her sidekick Yorkie, Coco, be able to solve the case?

A Flair for Beignets

With fabulous music, exquisite cuisine, and rich culture, how could a week in New Orleans be anything less than fantastic for Sadie Kramer and her sidekick Yorkie, Coco? And it is... until a customer at a popular patisserie drops dead face-first in a raspberry-almond tart. A competitive bakery, a newly formed friendship, and even her hotel's luxurious accommodations offer possible suspects. As Sadie sorts through a gumbo of interconnected characters, will she discover who the killer is, or will the killer discover her first?

A Flair for Truffles

Sadie Kramer's friendly offer to deliver three boxes of gourmet Valentines truffles for her neighbor's chocolate shop backfires when she arrives to find the intended recipient deceased. Even more intriguing is the fact that the elegant heart-shaped gifts were ordered by three different men. With the help of one detective and the hindrance of another, Sadie will search San Francisco for clues. But will she find out "whodunit" before the killer finds a way to stop her?

A Flair for Flip-Flops

When the body of a heartthrob celebrity washes up on the beach outside Sadie Kramer's luxury hotel suite, her fun in the sun soon turns into sleuthing with the stars. The resort's wine and appetizer gatherings, suspicious guest behavior, and casual strolls along the beach boardwalk may provide clues, but will they be enough to discover who the killer is, or will mystery and mayhem leave a Hollywood scandal unsolved?

A Flair for Goblins

When Sadie Kramer agrees to help decorate for San Francisco's high-society Halloween shindig, she expects to find whimsical ghosts, skeletons, and jack-o-lanterns when she shows up at the Wainwright Mansion, not a body. With two detectives, a paranormal investigator turned television star, and a cauldron full of family members cackling around her, Sadie and her sidekick Yorkie are determined to find out who the killer is. Will an old superstition help lead to the truth? Or will this simply become one more tale in the mansion's haunted history?

The Moonglow Christmas Series

Mistletoe at Moonglow

The small town of Timberton, Montana, hasn't been the same since resident chef and artist, Mist, arrived, bringing a unique new age flavor to the old western town. When guests check in for the holidays, they bring along worries, fears, and broken hearts, unaware that Mist has a way of working magic in people's lives. One thing is certain: no matter how cold winter's grip is on each guest, no one leaves Timberton without a warmer heart.

Silver Bells at Moonglow

Christmas brings an eclectic gathering of visitors and locals to the Timberton Hotel each year, guaranteeing an eventful season. Add in a hint of romance, and there's more than snow in the air around the small Montana town. When the last note of Christmas carols has faded away, the soft whisper of silver bells from the front door's wreath will usher guests and townsfolk back into the world with hope for the coming year.

Gingerbread at Moonglow

The Timberton Hotel boasts an ambiance of near-magical proportions during the Christmas season. As the aromas of ginger, cinnamon, nutmeg, and molasses mix with heartfelt camaraderie and sweet romance, holiday guests share reflections on family, friendship, and life. Will decorating the outside of a gingerbread house prove easier than deciding what goes inside?

Nutcracker Sweets at Moonglow

When a nearby theatre burns down just before Christmas, cast members of The Nutcracker arrive at the Timberton Hotel with only a sliver of holiday joy. Camaraderie, compassion, and shared inspiration combine to help at least one hidden dream come true. As with every Christmas season, this year's guests will face the New Year with a renewed sense of hope.

Snowfall at Moonglow

As holiday guests arrive at the Timberton Hotel with hopes of a white Christmas, unseasonably warm weather hints at a less-than-wintery wonderland. But whether the snow falls or not, one thing is certain: with resident artist and chef, Mist, around, there's bound to be a little magic. No one ever leaves Timberton without renewed hope for the future.

Yuletide at Moonglow

When a Yuletide festival promises jovial crowds, resident artist and chef, Mist, knows she'll have her hands full. Between the legendary Christmas Eve dinner at the Timberton Hotel and this season's festival events, the unique magic of Christmas in this small Montana town offers joy, peace, and community to guests and townsfolk alike. As always, no one will return home without a renewed sense of hope for the future.

Starlight at Moonglow

As the Christmas holiday approaches, a blizzard threatens the peaceful ambiance that the Timberton Hotel usually offers its guests. Even resident artist and chef, Mist, known to work near miracles, has no control over the howling winds and heavy snowfall. But there's always a bit of magic in this small Montana town, and this year's storm may just find it's no match for heartfelt camaraderie, joyful inspiration, and sweet romance.

Additional titles:

Cranberry Bluff

Molly Elliott's quiet life is disrupted when routine errands land her in the middle of a bank robbery. Accused and cleared of the crime, she flees both media attention and mysterious, threatening notes to run a bed and breakfast on the Northern California coast. Her new beginning is peaceful until five guests show up at the inn, each with a hidden agenda. As true motives become apparent, will Molly's past come back to haunt her, or will she finally be able to leave it behind?

Sweet Treats: Recipes from the Moonglow Christmas Series

Delicious recipes, including Glazed Cinnamon Nuts, Cherry Pecan Holiday Cookies, Chocolate Peppermint Bark, Cranberry Drop Cookies, White Christmas Fudge, Molasses Sugar Cookies, Lemon Crinkles, Spiced Apple Cookies, Swedish Coconut Cookies, Double Chocolate Walnut Brownies, Blueberry Oatmeal Cookies, Cocoa Kisses, Angel Crisp Cookies, Gingerbread Eggnog Trifle, Dutch Sour Cream Cookies, and more!

For more information on Deborah Garner's books:

Facebook: https://www.facebook.com/
deborahgarnerauthor
Twitter: https://twitter.com/PaigeandJake
Website: http://deborahgarner.com
Mailing list: http://bit.ly/deborahgarner

CPSIA information can be obtained
at www.ICGtesting.com
Printed in the USA
BVHW071206231121
622335BV00009B/273